Weatherfield Yesterday
The Cartwright Murders

D1458492

Weatherfield Yesterday
The Cartwright Murders

Ken Barlow
with Stephen Bennett

GRANADA
MEDIA

First published in 2000 by Granada Media
an imprint of André Deutsch Ltd
in association with
Granada Media Group
76 Dean Street
London W1V 5HA
www.vci.co.uk

A catalogue record for this book is available from the British Library

ISBN 0 233 99915 9

Typeset by Derek Doyle & Associates, Liverpool
Printed and bound in the UK by
Mackays of Chatham

1 3 5 7 9 10 8 6 4 2

Pictures reproduced courtesy of the Mary Evans Picture Library
appear on pages 21, 71, 83, 106
Photos from the author's collection,
pages 19, 22, 46, 56, 59, 92, 99, 110
Photographs reproduced courtesy of Granada Media,
pages 8, 13, 25, 36, 115

This work would have been impossible without the forbearance, understanding and love of my true and constant companion, Deirdre. When I have forgotten every other name in my History of Weatherfield, yours will remain.

PART 1

INTRODUCTION

After many years spent trawling for interesting material to fill a small, local newspaper, I've always known that the strangest stories can arise from the most innocuous enquiries. Nothing in my experience, however, led me to imagine that a spell of innocent probing into the origins of local street names would uncover the saga of passion, intrigue and brutal murder that was the remarkable 'Cut-throat Cartwright' Case and is now the subject of this small volume.

Looking into the general history of Weatherfield for my larger work on the subject, I had intended to include an appendix section on the naming of streets; why that particular name, when was it bestowed and so forth. Many of these names are self-explanatory, as evidenced by the turn of the century fashion for naming new blocks of streets after the great battles and resonant place names of the Boer War: Mafeking Street, Ladysmith Close and Transvaal Street being local examples. I then discovered that Victoria Street had been called Cartwright Street up until the end of the 1890s. Nothing strange in that, I assumed. Victoria Streets were springing up all over the place in the aftermath of the Diamond Jubilee and as the Queen's reign drew to an end. Oddly, though, it was the only street name in the entire area ever to have been changed, after its initial 'christening'. There were plenty of new streets that could have borne the name of the old queen – and what was wrong with 'Cartwright', anyway?

I'd imagined, correctly as it turned out, that the street must have been home to a coach and cart builder's workshop during the nineteenth century but then a period of research into the early cotton mills of the area revealed that many nearby streets were named after the philanthropic (so we are informed) owners of those forbidding, smoke-spewing giants that dominated the Weatherfield skyline for so long. Chapman Street still exists, as does Shaw Street and Raglan Street – all named after prominent local mill-owners. Yet the name Cartwright seemed to have been wiped from the slate of Weatherfield history for good. I had thought to include some light-hearted speculation in my 'History' as to the possible reasons for this, see if I might find a few local Cartwrights who would be prepared to reveal the odd, dark family secret – or even make one up with a view to establishing their own little urban legend for posterity.

That was when a search through Weatherfield Library's remarkable new computer database revealed far more than I'd bargained for. Local records and newspaper reports carried the grim truth of a scandal that had rocked the community all those years ago. The shame that had fallen upon the once-proud name of Cartwright during those last, sombre days of the old century was more than enough for local civic leaders and the shocked residents of those close-knit streets to wish the name washed clean out of Weatherfield memory for ever.

The following is an extract from the *Weatherfield Gazette* of 27 December 1897. It is the first record of what became known as the Cartwright Case. It also became the starting point for an investigation that throws new light on a dark footnote of Weatherfield's history.

Murder or Mischief?

A Mystery Either Way

A butcher's shop on Cartwright Street became the centre of a bizarre mystery yesterday. Police activity around the shop led to the rumour of foul play creeping among the inhabitants of the Cartwright Street area but Inspector Jack

Medlock of Weatherfield Constabulary, who is in charge of the case, refused to comment on an incident that apparently occurred some time over the Christmas period. However, this newspaper has learned from a source close to the events that the recent resident of the premises, Mr Nathaniel Bardsley, having not been seen since Christmas Day, was allegedly found dead on the morning of Boxing Day by a workmate, after what appear to have been circumstances of extreme violence. The mystery lies in the fact that when police arrived at the scene there was no sign of a body beyond a considerable quantity of what may or may not be human blood.

Despite Mr Medlock's unwillingness to expand publicly at this stage, the police appear to be treating the case as a murder enquiry, even though there would appear to be no victim present as of the time of this edition. The Gazette wonders whether our police force is not the victim of an elaborate and distasteful hoax.

This reporter has further been able to establish that a local man, Mr Thomas Sykes, an employee of Cartwright's Mill, thought to be the discoverer of the so-called dead body, is assisting police with their enquiries but is not believed to be a suspect.

The missing man is also an employee of Cartwright's. The owner of the shop, Mr Samuel Middleton, is said to be 'outraged and distressed'. We will pursue the story with great interest.

I was determined to do the same. The body was never found. This oddity in itself, I imagined, would make for an interesting paragraph or two in my 'History' but I hardly imagined that events would lead to the story taking over six months of my life.

History – in the form of documents, records and news-paper reports, as well as the received opinion lodged in the minds of many Weatherfield people – has offered us only one version of the Cartwright story and it goes as follows:

In the early hours of 26 December 1897, Bernard Cartwright, mill-owner and one of Weatherfield's leading citizens, slashed the throat of Nat Bardsley with a meat-cleaver then returned home and battered his wife, Alice, to death after discovering that she and Nat were lovers. Bernard admitted his guilt but never revealed the whereabouts of Nat's body. He was hanged for his crimes. Simple. Certainly, history settled for this version and has been happy with it for over a hundred years. I only had one question but it was the biggest and most demanding I could come up with – why? I began to dig further when I thought – wrongly – that the body had been found. The mystery only deepened.

Weatherfield – Early Spring 2000

I felt terrible. The whole thing was turning into a mess – probably of my own making. After the recent, horrific discovery of a decomposed body in premises being renovated on Victoria Street, I had done the last thing any sensible historian would contemplate and jumped to the wrong conclusions without checking the evidence. I had thought the body of Nat Bardsley had turned up at last and I had been proved completely, stupidly, wrong. The case remains *sub judice* but it soon became clear that this was not the body of the missing Cartwright victim as I had supposed. It was never my intention to re-open old wounds but certain local people, connected directly or otherwise to the Cartwright dynasty, naturally enough took offence. This led to an unfortunate series of misunderstandings and culminated with my sponsors – coincidentally those very people with Cartwright connections – withdrawing their support for my book. I am pleased to say that other means were found and publication was only briefly delayed but there was a time when I feared this story would never come to light.

As I sat at my front window watching the thin drizzle soak Coronation Street, I could see the work of many months disappearing, along with the rainwater, down the grid outside. The Cartwright story had gripped me and wouldn't let go. The more I looked at it, the more I was amazed by the number of contradictions and inaccuracies it contained. On the surface, newspapers and court records provided no more than a catalogue of confusion; the picture of what really happened coming through as little more than a blur. I became determined to blow away the fog that lingered over the few solid scraps of information I'd found. I think the answer has now emerged.

It's often when prospects look to have reached their lowest ebb that things can change. Fred Elliott – whose family history

Fred Elliott – master butcher and Weatherfield luminary. Surviving grandson of the notorious Bernard Cartwright.

is, in a way, the subject of this investigation and with whom I suffered the unfortunate falling out over sponsorship – came to the conclusion that the true story was what he wanted handing on to future generations of Elliotts, not some rag-bag of murky rumours that could be twisted into embarrassment for what is, after all, one of Weatherfield's most respected families. My research would not be set aside, after all. With Fred's willing compliance and the invaluable help and advice of many other friends and neighbours alike, the project was revived. The story can now be told in full and it starts like this . . .

Weatherfield – Winter, 1897

When Jack Medlock arrived at the back door of number thirteen Cartwright Street on that hard-frozen Boxing Day morning, the street had already begun to clear of its procession of workers on their way to the nearby mills. A confused and angry shop owner by the name of Samuel Middleton, a pale-looking Tommy Sykes and a grim-faced police constable stood waiting for him.

Medlock had picked up half the tale from the desk sergeant at the station and as the senior inspector on duty it was up to him to go and see what all the fuss was about.

There was blood, all right. Plenty of it. Mostly dry now but still sticky in patches at the bottom of the stairs where it must have run down and gathered in the dark pool that had now been spread further by what looked like Tommy's boot prints. But that was all. There was no sign of any dead body. Medlock now doubted Tommy's story in favour of his own instant theory involving a drunken, festive stunt in rather poor taste – this was a butcher's, after all – and said so in no uncertain terms. It was too cold to stand around playing games.

Tommy Sykes was aghast. To his complete amazement and in the half hour or so it had taken to run to the police station, pant out his story and drag a wary constable along

14

with him, roping in the shop's proprietor on the way, it seemed that his one-time pal Nat Bardsley had vanished.

Jack Medlock was an interesting man, although, unlike Sherlock Holmes, he had no talent for the violin and was never a denizen of Victorian Weatherfield's opium establishments – not that such a thing could ever have existed north of Watford, surely. Jack's vices, such as they were, involved a pint too many on occasion, a ready song in a surprisingly pure tenor voice and, it was rumoured, a rather injudicious fascination with illegal pugilism that ran counter to his chosen profession of Police Inspector.

Jack had 'contacts', it was said. Lots of them and on both sides of the law. Some thought this made him untrustworthy. Others knew that it was what made him such a remarkably effective copper and, at thirty-six, the same age as Bernard Cartwright, a favourite with the ordinary men on the force. It was also said that, if arrest couldn't be avoided, the majority of locals villains always felt that bit less put out if it were Jack wielding the cuffs.

His love of the fight game was widely acknowledged and it was not only as a spectator that Jack was renowned. A small-built man, he'd nevertheless been something of a brawler in his youth and it was not unheard of for a bloody and battered Jack Medlock to drag an unconscious crook into the station by his shirt collar having previously explained the benefits of the man accompanying him to the station quietly and then found his wisdom and generosity questioned.

Jack was a bachelor at the time of the murders, highly eligible in the eyes of local society, no doubt, just as Bernard had been. He was also, like Bernard, a Square-Dealer – a fact that would have a resounding significance on the eventual outcome of their story.

That morning, 26 December 1897, Jack Medlock was baffled. The man Sykes, though no great intellect, had no trouble sticking to the same story, in detail, over and over again. Yet where was the body? Where was this victim, so graphically described and, apparently, so clearly evident not three quarters of an hour earlier. In search of fresh air, Jack must have emerged from the blood-caked stairwell and into the shadow of Cartwright's cotton mill opposite, wondering just where to begin unravelling the threads of the mystery. The answer was closer than he could have imagined.

Photographs prove, and all agreed at the time, that Alice Rafferty was a rare, red-headed beauty. She was the only daughter of Irish parents who had arrived from Cork, looking for work, ten years earlier. She was the only girl in the house but Alice had seven brothers, so she was used to looking out for herself and could, reputedly, express an opinion in language that would have made many a sailor blush. She'd had a temper as a young girl and her brothers would have thought twice before crossing her. Alice was independent, intelligent and vivacious and it was no surprise that when Bernard Cartwright first saw her, leaning across the carding machines, probably laughing with her workmates over some risqué remark at the expense of one of the shop-floor lads, his heart was no longer his own.

She was twenty-three when they married in the spring of 1896. He was thirty-five, the inheritor of a prosperous and growing cotton mill from a Liverpudlian father who'd made a healthy pile in imports and exports, and already the father of two young sons from a previous marriage. All we know of Bernard's first wife, Elisabeth, is that she died of consumption at the age of twenty-nine, leaving him to bring up the two boys, Robert and William, without her, if not quite alone. He benefited greatly from the ministrations of a live-in governess, Beryl Baines, who, it was said, never at any time got on with the second Mrs Cartwright. Letters still within the family record that Elisabeth's death left Bernard shattered and the openness and generosity of spirit he was known for became hidden under a cloak of deep and protracted mourning. Hidden, that is, until the light from the laughing, brown eyes of a beautiful Irish factory hand blazed straight through the darkness of the past and, in the view of all who knew him, gave Bernard a renewed sense of purpose.

Some of the newspaper accounts of Bernard and Alice's wedding retain a slightly sniffy tone. Beneath the detailed descriptions of the lavish spread and the bride's cream taffeta, lay the question many were asking, albeit in hushed tones: what was this wealthy and highly eligible local bachelor doing chasing after a flighty Irish girl from the carding room? It was simple. Bernard was besotted and from then on, whether it was in a theatre, park or civic reception, Alice was always at home and always the focus of every eye. The reason men were drawn to her was the same reason women kept their distance.

And yet, we know that Alice retained her popularity at work. She had many friends who still spoke highly of her – some at Bernard's trial – even after she'd exchanged the factory floor for the master's parlour. They said she never changed, was always the same laughing, sparkling Alice with the cheeky look in her eye. Maybe that was where things started to go wrong.

By the time the winter of 1897 came around, in the second year of their marriage, Alice had become the proud, doting mother of a baby girl, Amelia, while Bernard's ever-expanding business interests now meant that he'd need to take on a new foreman at Cartwright's.

The man he appointed was a good-looking, local jack-the-lad; a well-known amateur footballer, pigeon-fancier and hard drinker. A man by the name of Nat Bardsley.

The Cartwrights, Bernard and Alice, with their two sons and new-born daughter, lived in a big, smart town-house that still stands on the edge of what is now the Red Rec on the outskirts of Weatherfield. The planned wide-open, green space so

beloved of Victorian developers, allowed easy access for the
young family to promenade and take the air of a summer's
evening whenever the fancy took them. Not that the
Weatherfield air of the 1890s could ever be imagined as clean
or fresh with the sheer volume of factory filth belched out into
it on a daily basis. My own mother recalled, as a child in the
1920s, lifting up from her pillow in the morning to see a ghostly
outline of her own head preserved on the clean linen after a
fine film of black grime had settled on the cloth around it. It is
little wonder that chronic respiratory illness was rife
throughout the area in those days and for many years after.
On a weekend in the park, nevertheless, it was said if you sat
around long enough, the whole town would pass by.

Alice would sit on a bench, the baby Amelia beside her in
the most expensive pram the town's merchants could
provide, and watch Bernard and the two little boys play
cricket against a tree trunk. They must have appeared the
perfect family group to any who saw them. One who saw
them often and couldn't help but admire as he passed
through the park with his mates on their way to the football
pitches, was Nat Bardsley. Tommy Sykes remembered him
call out to Bernard on one occasion, asking, 'Any jobs going,
yet, Mr Cartwright? I'm a good grafter, me, tha knows.'

'I'll let you know as soon as there is, Nat, don't worry, lad,'
had been Bernard's reply.

But Nat's boldness proved to have a dual purpose. It meant
he could get a closer look at the red-headed beauty on the
bench and make certain, in his customary cocksure way, that
she got a good look at him.

This kind of encounter occurred more than once and we
can be fairly certain that Alice did indeed get a good look at
Nat and, though she would always remain coolly aloof in
public, that she liked what she saw.

Tommy Sykes remembered those early encounters between
Alice and his friend Nat. At Bernard's trial for the double

Nat Bardsley, showing the style that impressed the ladies.

murder, he told the judge how he'd walked through the park on Sunday morning with Nat and the rest of the lads on their way to play football and Nat had made no bones about the alternative athletic activity he'd like to indulge in with the haughty-looking Mrs Cartwright. Every man gave Alice a second, sidelong glance, Tommy said, in the hope of some small favour but to his knowledge, none had ever had that glance returned in any significant way. Except Nat. Yet for all Nat's bluff, or otherwise, regarding his prowess with the ladies, there came a time when he wouldn't be drawn on the subject of Alice. Tommy observed that Nat's laddish speculations had stopped quite suddenly and from around that same time he began to notice that his pal no longer welcomed 'comments of a lewd nature' at work or play from fellow mill hands or team-mates. Nat once 'dished out a right back-hander' to a workmate who'd gone a bit too far as Alice passed by. Even then, in Tommy's view, nobody suspected. Throughout that time, most people believed that Nat was 'carrying on' with someone else, anyway – another married woman by the name of Annie Collier, who worked in accounts. But that was Nat, the way he was, and if he'd had a barney with a mate one minute, he'd be buying him a pint the next. He treated everyone he met the same way, according to Tommy: straight. And he expected the same, or nothing, from them.

Bernard Cartwright liked Nat Bardsley. He was under no illusions as to the lad's nature and Bernard hadn't risen to the heights he now commanded without being able to spot a rogue when he saw one. As a manager, too, Bernard was no fool. He reckoned that if there was a popular jack-the-lad on the work force, it was always better to have him with you than against you. If hard choices had to be made on the shop floor, bad news was always better received by the workers from 'one of their own' than from the bosses. Not that Bernard was seen as a tyrannical employer – far from it – but he preferred his workers to see changes in the workplace, whether it be modernizations, lay-offs or increased hours for no more pay, as unavoidable. That's why, in the November of 1897, Nat Bardsley was finally rewarded with the job he'd long craved – foreman at Cartwright's.

Nat became the acceptable buffer between Bernard and the employees. He revelled in the responsibility, the elevated status and the extra pay that enabled him to buy the white silk scarves that, in a nod to the traditions of his early working days down the pit, he always wore with a Cyrano-like panache.

Hedley Fitton's famous 'Weatherfield Saturday Night' (1894),
currently on display in the Public Library.

Nat Bardsley was born in Manchester in 1866, just as that city was returning to the settled trading relationship with America that was to bring great wealth to the likes of Bernard Cartwright in later years. He never knew his parents. The unnamed, unknown baby could have been no more than three months old when he was found by Annie Bardsley, already, at twenty-eight, a mother of six, on the steps of an Ancoats workhouse. Although no recorded explanation remains, he was probably taken in on the grounds that one more wouldn't make much difference.

Apart from the blanket he was wrapped in, the child brought no possessions to his new life except for a gold

The young Bernard Cartwright, dressed for a wedding in 1877.

charm on a string found in the bottom of the wooden box in which he lay. It was an Egyptian good luck symbol, the kind that Annie and her husband Frank had seen worn by the gypsies who regularly passed through the town. This later came to explain the boy's dark good looks and carefree spirit and young Nat used to enjoy speculating on his true origins as the lost prince of some romantic Ruritanian kingdom or the product of the secret union of royalty and a Spanish burlesque dancer. The truth was almost certainly more mundane in that Nat was one of many babies who suffered a similar fate in those days. He was simply luckier than most and he grew up, thanks to the good offices of Annie and Frank, into an athletic and high-spirited young man whose excesses were invariably forgiven in the face of a winning combination of charm and cheek. For all the head-shaking that surrounded Nat's adventures, everyone agreed on one thing: the lad didn't have a malicious bone in his body.

Alice Rafferty, it seems, would have generated sexual tension in a frozen corpse. She knew she had the power to turn men's thoughts as well as their heads and it was said in her defence that the less she tried, the more her irresistible, silken magnetism exerted its pull. Most described her as 'a lovely girl' while acknowledging that apparently sane and sober men would turn to a lascivious jelly in her presence. Those women who didn't know her, of course, hated her for this. Alice didn't care. She'd never chased men – never needed to – and she'd never stolen a man from another woman. Those closest to her said that, with Alice, in spite of what others might have suspected, it had to be love, complete and uncon- ditional, or nothing. This being the case, we can only imagine that the passion she began to feel for Nat Bardsley in the final months of her life tore her apart with guilt as she entered into that fateful betrayal of her husband and children, unable to deny her own heart.

Bernard Cartwright, in contrast, grew up a quiet and

studious lad. He was never one to give his parents any undue sleepless nights over his riotous behaviour around the town or have irate fathers beating a path to his door, trailing their dishonoured daughters behind them. He seems to have been the ideal heir to the Cartwright empire: honest, serious, trustworthy and, it seems, dependably dull as a child. Though Bernard's education was important to him and his family – and records show the young man did well at school without demonstrating any startling intellectual prowess – his father brought him into the factory at the first opportunity. The lad took to it like a duck to water. He loved the incessant clatter and rumble of productivity, the awesome beauty of the machines and the sheer vitality of the work force. It wasn't long before Bernard could turn his hand to just about any task in the place. He knew how the machines worked from the inside out and so knew how to fix them. A big, strong lad, he was never afraid of getting his hands dirty. He learned the secrets of cotton; its properties, its glories and its annoying little habits. He was never too proud to ask the simplest questions of the hyper-efficient, no-nonsense women on the 'shoddy' or the hard-to-impress old boys who serviced the machines. He grew close to their problems, gripes and short-cuts and it made him a better boss. He gained experience and perhaps more importantly, he gained respect. He gradually grew into the task and into his own self-confident and assured manhood. Bernard Cartwright had found his true vocation.

It's time we went for a walk. I have been indebted during the compilation of this brief account to the invaluable contribution of my friend and neighbour, Roy Cropper. Roy is a stalwart member of the Weatherfield Historical Society and was responsible for unearthing the buried seed of a possible solution to the mystery of what really happened to those involved in the Cartwright murders. More of that later.

Roy took me on a most congenial guided tour of what

Weatherfield historian and café owner, Roy Cropper.

remains of 'Old Weatherfield', in search of the background to our tale. So much of Victorian Weatherfield has disappeared in recent years and for that we must be thankful. I wish I could report that the modern planners had replaced the crumbling terraces with a brighter vision but that would be difficult.

We started on our own Coronation Street, one of the few

terraces that remain proudly intact, with a view to ending up, full circle, if you will, on Victoria Street – Cartwright Street that was – having mapped out as much as we could trace of the ground on which the drama was played out.

A Freschco's supermarket now stands on part of the ground that was once occupied by Cartwright's Mill. Roy showed me the remains of the old gates that can still be located at one end of what is now a bleak and charmless car-parking area, dotted with stray shopping trolleys that the local children seem to be able to conjure from thin air no matter how conscientiously the things are corralled. Again, though, that's another story, albeit it one close to my own heart, as readers of my *Gazette* column will no doubt be aware. But I digress.

It's still quite easy to imagine, standing there between the two tired stone blocks that represent all that remains of those great gates, the stark grandeur of what was once one of the North-west's mightiest temples of commerce; one of the ever-churning engine rooms that generated the wealth of empire. In the 1890s, Cartwright's employed nearly 600 souls. If the Lancashire cotton industry, based round Manchester, was, as often boasted, the centre of the universe, then Cartwright's was a glowing particle in that nucleus. It must have seemed then, like Ozymandias's desert monument, that those massive cotton-palaces would stand forever, that the commercial and military might of Great Britain was unassailable, that the rest of the world – which no doubt had its occasional uses – trembled, and that God was in His heaven and all was right with the world.

Back then, there was no inkling that within two generations, three at most, the cotton would be gone, taking the jobs and the factories with it. This left the still proud but confused local people to scrape and scratch an existence until the great provider that was the cotton industry could be replaced by the myriad new technologies and service industries that, we hope, will keep the working heart of Weatherfield beating on, far into the twenty-first century and beyond.

Roy painted the picture for me – of head-scarved women bantering across the 'shoddy' belts, of the clatter of the carding room and the play of light and dust across the great vault of the work space, of the glittering, rocket-speed shuttles, criss-crossing their elaborate frames like jungle birds flashing from branch to branch. And the deafening noise, the constant, glorious clamour of success, the stomach-fluttering hum that told all who entered the place that this was all just one big machine, alive, breathing and, above all, constantly working. For all its awesome power and back-breaking drudgery, there must have been a strange reassurance about those places; a security that many aspects of life at the turn of that new century could never provide. As a child, I remember standing in the magical grip of one such factory, watching my grandmother and her friends at work, all covered in the floating white 'bits' that filled the air as if in the aftermath of the world's best ever pillow-fight; the women's rough hands flying with total certainty in some arcane ritual skill far beyond my childish understanding, their voices lifted high above the din. I was spellbound. Roy's account of a day-to-day workings of Cartwright's brought it all back.

We moved on towards the canal. They're restoring it now. Les Battersby, one of my near neighbours, has been involved in the work and I'm indebted to him for a number of entertaining anecdotes regarding the canal's history – sadly, not all of which I am able repeat here, if only in the interests of propriety. Part of the Bridgewater Canal system, the Weatherfield section will soon become one of the renovated linking waterways that will serve the activity holiday market. It will doubtless boast a cosmetic charm that will remind us of a slower, gentler time. In reality, and in Bernard Cartwright's day, it was a busy, dirty thoroughfare; a polluted vein feeding into the main artery that was the Manchester Ship Canal and carrying an immense weight of first barge and then far bigger sea-going traffic to Liverpool and all points beyond –

to the Americas, the West Indies, India, China, Australia and back.

It was on the banks of this canal that one of the key events in our mystery took place. It was here that Jack Medlock apprehended Bernard Cartwright after a chase that began in the depths of Bernard's own factory. It was here that the two men had the short conversation that shaped later events and gave us our perception, misguided or otherwise, of the so-called facts of the case.

Let's look for a moment at a section of the front page story from the *Weatherfield Gazette* of 4 January 1898. Beneath the headline, 'Mill Owner Charged With Cruel Double Murder' we go on to read that *'Inspector Jack Medlock apprehended his man on the banks of the Bridgewater Canal, where it runs through Weatherfield, only after a desperate chase and a violent struggle. Cartwright is believed to have acknowledged his guilt there and then in the presence of a number of officers.'* If only the reality behind those simple, supposed facts was so straightforward.

The old canal is looking tired in places. The fruits of restoration have yet to blossom and one is still more likely to see an abandoned pram than a gaily-painted narrow boat. Roy informed me, as we walked, that the Romans built the first waterway into Weatherfield as a link between their settlement (recently discovered under the Red Rec) and the Irwell and the Irk (the latter river still runs, remarkably for it is almost completely hidden, through the centre of Manchester).

Roy told me of the Weatherfield Mudlarks, who would eke out a meagre existence by trawling the banks of the canal and the nearby rivers and streams for any old tat that could be turned into money – bits of cloth, coal, metal, anything they could lay their hands on or get to before the rats did. The most famous of their number was one Ned Bancroft, a registered rat-catcher and sometime highwayman of the eighteenth century who ruled the Weatherfield underworld in the manner of a MacHeath or a Jack Ketch.

I also learned more of the discovery of a Viking war helmet in a silted-up backwater in 1956, that proved once and for all that the Norsemen had raided far up into the heart of Lancashire from the Irish Sea. The fearsome, jewel-encrusted artefact now resides in the Viking Museum in York and is believed to be one of the finest surviving examples of its kind anywhere in the world. I sometimes wonder whether, if we could only delve back that far, there's a blond-haired, blue-eyed Weatherfielder owing half his or her genetic make-up to a Norseman who stayed behind, ensnared by the charms of a local village beauty.

The canal has an important part to play in our story and we will return to it later.

From the mouth of the tunnel that takes a stretch of the canal under the hill at one end of Weatherfield's largest common-land area, the Red Rec, and the very spot where Bernard Cartwright was run to ground, Roy and I turned off to explore the last remaining quarter of Weatherfield that looks today as it must have done then. The street lamps are modern, granted, and the cars that adorn the fronts of the houses would not have been there, but to all intents and purposes, the little enclave made up of the likes of Rosamund Street, Inkerman Street, Victoria, Mafeking and Coronation Street stands to this day as a solid reminder of a time gone by.

Victoria Street, Cartwright Street that was, is now distinguished from its neighbours by a row of smart new shops: a hardware store, a taxi rank and ironically, a butcher's that in a bizarre historical coincidence, is now run by Fred Elliott and Ashley Peacock, both the direct descendants – grandson and great-grandson respectively – of Bernard Cartwright. I reveal this with the full cooperation, insistence even, of these two gentlemen in the fullest confidence that no macabre, speculative associations will link them or their admirable business practice to their unfortunate ancestor!

It was on the site of these restored premises that Tommy

Sykes stumbled upon his horrific discovery over a hundred years ago. Roy and I stood on the opposite side of the street and tried to recapture the feel of those days when this was Cartwright Street. It had the workshop at one end, that much we know; a kind of late-nineteeth century garage and repair shop, and photographs we unearthed from the period clearly show the little shop-front that hid the murder from the world outside. It is fascinating to speculate that one of the figures in that faded image could be one of the players in our drama. Picture, too, as we did, that street in the grip of winter and from a side-alley, picture the muffled figure of Bernard Cartwright emerging into the frozen morning with Nat Bardsley's blood on his hands.

We went on to visit the library in the centre of Weatherfield, taking with us what we knew: that on the morning of the 12 April 1898, Bernard Cartwright was hanged at Preston Assizes for the double murder of his wife, Alice, and Nat Bardsley. The body of the latter was never found. The officer in charge of the investigation was one Jack Medlock, to whom Bernard's confession was finally made, and the case was, in the common parlance of such matters, open and shut. Mr Justice Roberts condemned what all saw as 'a barbaric and savage act of jealous revenge, carried out by a man driven to madness by suspicions of his wife's infidelity.' The murderer was reported to have accepted the verdict with a quiet dignity that marked his behaviour throughout the short trial. The wife was shown to have died from massive head injuries and Cartwright, though he would never reveal the whereabouts of the body, confirmed that Nat Bardsley's death was caused by a knife-wound to the throat.

And yet the question remained – what happened to Nat's body? And why the scene described earlier in which Medlock and the others found nothing but a blood-stained floor? Bernard freely admitted to the murder so why move the body and then deny a certain knowledge of its subsequent whereabouts? Something clearly didn't sit right. One thing that struck me as I sat poring over the contemporary documents, long after Roy had left me to my research that day and the library was near to closing, was Jack Medlock's virtual disappearance from reports and records of the case, after the conviction. Oddly, there seemed almost nothing from him at the trial – one brief but significant moment is recorded here in a later chapter – or in the aftermath of the arrest. The *Weatherfield Gazette* was only, grudgingly, able to report his reluctance to be drawn on the details of the case. It seemed strange.

It was then, by a complete accident, that I made a remarkable discovery. Coincidentally, the Medlock is one of the many rivers that links to that same network that incorporates the Bridgewater Canal. Having spent much of the day discussing the local waterways and feeling frustrated by the seeming dead-end to the mystery of the missing corpse, I decided to investigate the library's 'new baby' – long overdue – a state-of-the-art computer database. Finding material that would serve to inform my larger 'History' of the town, I printed off reams on the Irwell, the Irk, the Ship Canal, sadly less on the Bridgewater Canal and on other miscellaneous items. It then occurred to me that I'd left out the Medlock that winds down from the Pennines through Oldham and Ashton. I typed in the word. Some bits and pieces of interest came up – early industrial settlements, site of early water pump and the like. The computer though, blessedly free of human logic and listing any and all Medlocks in its memory, threw up an admittedly short list of books not only with that word in the title but with 'Medlock' as the author's name, on subjects from rock formations to Romantic poetry. And there it was, almost certainly the only copy anywhere in the public domain. A book I had no idea, until that moment, had ever been written. The missing link in the puzzle and, I believe, the key to the Cartwright mystery: *Just A Bobby's Job* (Salford University Press, 1923) – the memoirs of Detective Inspector Jack Medlock.

*

Jack Medlock's book proved to be a revelation and, in the account of the Cartwright Case, as much in what seemed to have been omitted as in what was actually there. Although it's no longer in print and cannot now be taken from the library building, I would recommend it as a fascinating insight into the mind of a complex man. The bulk of the work centres around an exhaustive account of the more famous Monsall Vampire Case of 1904/5 (cf. also *The Golden Age of British Detection* ed Mather and Platt, Methuen, 1954, also, alas, out of print) which became something of a career high-point for Jack. What is surprising is how little of the book is devoted to the Cartwright Case yet the author seems unable to push it completely out of his mind, constantly referring back to it as 'that unfortunate business', or to Bernard as a man caught up in 'the grip of a tragic fate'. Other villains get short shrift. Jack had no qualms about sending any criminal, man or women, to gaol or even gallows, if the evidence showed they were guilty, yet with Bernard, there is a different note struck – a note, almost, of regret. What follows is a brief extract – describing the day of Bernard's execution – that might convey something of the tone:

> *'I walked by the canal that same evening and passed the very spot where my men had run him to ground. I stood for a moment in thought, as I had on that very day of the arrest, and recalled my brief exchange of words with that pitiable man whose life had been forfeit to the noose only a few hours earlier; and of everything he'd told me afterwards, of how his life had been transformed into that singular nightmare from which only the hangman could release him. He had his wish now; the nightmare was over and for better or worse, I had played my small part.'*

I was struck by the sheer oddness of these sentiments. 'For better or worse'? And what of the nightmare of the two victims? It was from these early passages in the book that my investigation of the story truly began and it was from these first signs that I began to follow the path to my own attempt to recreate, in later chapters, the events of the murder, the aftermath and Jack Medlock's unorthodox role in the whole tragic business.

It took me two days to finish reading the book. The clues were there but I was unable to figure out what they meant. Then it struck me; something I'd missed in all the fog that surrounded the Cartwright story. As I walked home past the old factory gates once more, I was suddenly struck by a passage that occurs towards the end of the book. I had been trying to imagine the shock-wave of rumour and scandal that must have swept through that factory community a hundred years ago, before radio and television, when many of Cartwright's work-force probably couldn't even read the newspaper. It struck me how much weight would have been contained in and ascribed to the words people actually said; what they passed on to each other and how it would be interpreted, reshaped even, as it was passed on again and again. The passage from Medlock's writings suddenly made sense.

'I may have made many mistakes and been guilty of arrogance and stubbornness during the long course of my career. I may even have bent the occasional rule in the removal of an unsavoury reprobate or two from the streets of Weatherfield. But of one thing, though the outcome still pains me, I am absolutely sure in my own mind; I always dealt square with Bernard Cartwright.'

Why should the outcome have caused Jack so much pain? The 'outcome' not the crime. And then there was that last sentence 'dealt square'. I needed to follow the arrow Jack had left that surely pointed to the truth. Both Jack and Bernard were Square Dealers. Somehow, I was convinced, their 'brotherhood' had been highly significant to the outcome of the case.

The Square Dealers is a quasi-Masonic organization that still thrives to this day in the old industrial heartlands of the North. Nowadays its function is similar to that of the Round Tables or Lions Clubs, where prominent members of the community meet socially and initiate philanthropic works on behalf of those less fortunate than themselves. All these organizations have their arcane lore, tracing their origins or blueprint back to Ancient Egypt, Babylon, Byzantium or some such. Many also have their peculiar handshakes, their initiation ceremonies and their codes of conduct and secrecy. The Square Dealers certainly keep their membership secret and a place among their ranks is offered only by invitation from within.

The organization was founded in 1882 by a group of mill owners and its membership was opened to local dignitaries – all male, a 'distinction' that holds to this day – and all, it was said, 'principled Christian gentlemen of influence and good standing within the community'. An anonymous but reliable source consented to look through the society's secret records and revealed to me that Bernard Cartwright was introduced to the society by his father and became an active member of the Weatherfield group throughout the 1890s. The nearest neighbouring lodge was in Salford, where, apparently, there was also a welcome in the ranks for policemen. Sometime in the late 1880s, Jack Medlock accepted that welcome.

The same source informs me that a Square Dealer is bound by the code of his order to 'deal square' with his fellows above all else. Short of a direct flouting of the laws of the land, this means that corners may be cut, paths cleared and information revealed or buried according to necessity, in favour of fellow Dealers wherever possible. To call this a grey area would be a huge understatement. Often, I'm told, the law has been circumvented, if not actually broken, in instances in which members have seen their own interpreta-

tion of 'right and just' fall slightly to one side of the legal position. Such is the way, I'm sure, with many such bastions of
influence. Still . . . I needed to know more.

Medlock's book makes mention, of course, of his own family.
He married in 1902 – a local woman named Rose Tanner –
and the couple had four children. In a breathless search
through parish records and amid silent prayers to the gods of
longevity, I discovered that one of the siblings, Martha, born
in 1910, was still alive and living in Weatherfield at the age of
eighty-nine. I had, I fervently hoped, forged a living link with
the past and with my mystery.

The name Martha Medlock, to quote W.C. Fields, struck me
as a 'euphonious appellation'. Unfortunately, though not for
the lady herself, of course, she'd married a man called
Cribbins and the magic now seemed ever-so-slightly
tarnished. I'm not sure who or what I expected as I waited in
the drizzling rain outside the smart, dark green front door of
that little terraced house on Inkerman Street. What I could
never have hoped for was the sprightly, opinionated, wickedly
flirtatious and completely lucid little woman who greeted me
warmly and showed me into her neat living room with its
lovingly-preserved antimacassars, its family china behind
glass and its framed photographs of generations past, all
kept under the surveillance of the single hooded eye of an
enormous, ancient and perennially-bored cat called Baggins.

Once I'd extricated myself from the dubious delights of the
Baggins Body-Search and settled down in the armchair with
a cup and saucer, it was all I could do to keep my attention
focused on Martha, warming up her memory and recovering
stories like old linen teacloths from a drawer, rather than
gaze around the room looking for pictures of Jack. They were
there, and in number – Jack in uniform, Jack laughing with the
family on the front at Blackpool, as The Great Detective in a
severe portrait that I knew the *Gazette* had used more than
once – but they would have to wait. First, I had a thousand

questions. Or so it seemed. If I'd had that many, in fact, I'd still be there now as I soon discovered that Martha loved to talk and once she was launched into a topic, she was almost impossible to stop.

I learned of her childhood and of Weatherfield during both wars, yet Martha was never drawn into a lament for a bygone

Young heir to the Cartwright legacy, Ashley Peacock.

The Cartwright Murders

age. As far as she was concerned, life had become easier
and easier as the twentieth century progressed and her chief
regret was that she felt too old to take advantage of all the
luxuries we 'young 'uns' take for granted.

I also learned about her father; the highly-respected public
figure who 'liked a drink' a little too much on occasion, the
masterly detective who walked close to the edge of the criminal underworld and the peaceable, loving family man who
was fascinated by violence.

I was captivated by Martha's tales. She regaled me with
anecdotes from her long life, revealing a deep love for her
'fayther' that had clearly never dimmed over the years since
his death, aged seventy-six, in 1948. She told me the whereabouts of Jack's grave, which I resolved to visit and which is
described in a later chapter. She gave me new names to
research from her father's many associations, colleagues
and villains alike. She put faces to some of those names that
I only knew from references I'd passed over in the court
records and the newspaper reports. I would go back to them
with renewed interest. Initially, however, Martha seemed to
know little of the Cartwright story. It all happened long before
she was born, after all.

It was during my third visit, when I'd finally earned a certain
grudging degree of acceptance from Baggins, that Martha,
in her chirpy, matter-of-fact way as she poured the tea,
dropped her bomb-shell.

"Course, *probably never even did it.'*

I was confused. The comment had come completely out of the
blue as Martha was returning from a search of the kitchen for
the Rich Teas.

'I beg your pardon?' I replied. Curious.

*'Cartwright. He probably didn't do it. So me father thought,
any road. He were knockin' on then, mind. Retired from*

*police long since. And there were no point asking him more
after that, 'cos he'd tell you nowt else.'*

Where to go from here? Martha's assertion that her father
suspected Bernard Cartwright was a wronged man now had
my head spinning with possibilities. Jack Medlock was the
officer in charge of the case. How could circumstances have
led to Bernard's execution if the man in possession of a
means of saving him – an honest man of undoubted integrity
– had not chosen to do so? I went back to the court records.

The Council for the Prosecution in the trial of Bernard
Cartwright was a man by the name of Samuel Chapman. As
the defendant had made a plea of guilty to both counts of
murder, Chapman didn't have to work too hard to build up the
case for the Crown. However, he was known as a man with a
taste for the theatrical and in his summation of the case,
apparently a virtual one-man-show of re-enactment worthy of
an Oscar in itself, he reminded the jury of the breathless
chase along the canal that had led to Bernard's apprehension and arrest.

Jack Medlock had been accompanied by a sergeant and
two uniformed constables. One of the constables, a PC
Whittaker, had submitted this account of the final moments of
the chase. I read through it twice, then a third time, in order
to confirm what I felt sure was the pivotal moment in the fate
of Bernard Cartwright.

*'I was first to him, just before he could get into the
tunnel. If he'd gone another ten yards we might have
lost him in the dark. He was quick for a big man and
he'd already jumped a lock to get across the canal. I
grabbed his coat but I fell. There was a bit of a
scramble and I thought I'd lost him. After that I don't
know what happened exactly but I sensed the others
had caught up. Somebody jumped over me and pinned
Cartwright against the wall at the mouth of the tunnel.*

I realized it was Mr Medlock and by the time I'd picked myself up they were having a right old set to. Mr Medlock shouted something like, "Give it up, man," then something strange happened and we all just stood, like we'd forgotten why we were there. From going at it like a lunatic one minute Cartwright just stopped and looked straight at Mr Medlock. He said something but I couldn't make it out properly. He called him "Jack", I know that much, so you had to give him credit for his cheek. There was a pause for what seemed like an age but could not have been more than a few seconds. I tried to go closer but Mr Medlock held out his hand as if to say, "it's all right, you can stay back". Then I heard him say to Cartwright, "Aye, I will". That's all. And they just stood there looking at one another. After that, Cartwright came with us like we were leading a lamb back to its pen. It was like he was settled in himself to whatever was going to happen. We never had a minute's trouble with him after that.'

I immediately searched through the records of Jack Medlock's testimony and came to the relevant section, describing the same moments; a passage of question and answer between Chapman and the inspector himself.

Chapman: *You exchanged words with Mr Cartwright immediately upon his apprehension. Would that be correct?*
Medlock: *Yes, sir.*
Chapman: *Can you recall the exact words that were exchanged?*
Medlock: *At which particular moment?*
Chapman: *Your men have speculated that Cartwright admitted his guilt to you upon realizing that escape was no longer a possibility. Hence his subsequent willingness to accompany you without further struggle.*
Medlock: *My men are not the world's best when it comes to*

speculation, sir. I prefer them to leave that to me as it is often safer.

Chapman (amid sounds of general amusement within the court): *Nevertheless, Inspector…*

Medlock: *Nevertheless…we did exchange words, sir, as you say. Yes.*

Chapman: *And would you be so kind as to share these words with the court?*

Medlock: *Mr Cartwright asked me for assurance that he would be treated fairly.*

Chapman: *Is that all?*

Medlock: *That is all, sir. I assured him that wherever it lay within my power, he would be.*

I was fascinated by the character of Medlock that these few exchanges presented. The policeman's due respect for the surroundings of the court was clearly there but so too was the irreverent wit. Medlock's men, by all accounts, were fiercely loyal to their boss, so his little jibe must have carried enough warmth to show that this was just an example of the banter of a hard and close-knit team. But more than this, I was fascinated by those few words, *'Mr Cartwright asked me for assurance that he would be treated fairly'*. And then there was PC Whittaker's assertion that in making this request, Bernard, in an act of what the constable saw as 'cheek', had called Medlock by his christian name.

Bernard Cartwright knew, as he fled the factory on the day of his arrest, who his prospective nemesis was. Medlock's own writings hint to it. The two had never met but their paths had certainly crossed on at least one previous occasion. In the desperation of the chase through Weatherfield that led to Bernard's capture, the mill owner held tight in his mind to the one card he had left to play, the knowledge that Jack Medlock was a fellow Square Dealer.

'….assurance that he would be treated fairly.'

How would Bernard have put that in his own words? *'Promise me you will treat me fairly, Jack'*? Is it not more likely, under the circumstances, and in the light of what followed, that Bernard's actual words were more likely to have been, in the accepted argot of their brotherhood,

'Will you deal square with me, Jack?'

And Whittaker had clearly heard the reply – measured and solemn as it must have been – again, as I have subsequently learned, using the accepted ritual response,

'Aye. I will.'

From that moment on, the stakes in the Cartwright affair were changed for ever.

At this point I settled on a different approach. As I began to amass further information I could see that the mire of hints and ambiguities was only getting thicker and harder to navigate at every turn. I once more set out those pieces of the puzzle that I knew, or was now sufficiently convinced, to hold true.

1. Nat Bardsley was murdered and his body was never found. Bernard Cartwright admitted the murder and corroborated the evidence of Tommy Sykes that the man died as a result of having his throat cut.
2. Alice Cartwright died from a lethal blow to the side of the head, administered, on his own admission, by her husband Bernard Cartwright.
3. Jack Medlock belonged to the same secret society as Bernard Cartwright.
4. Bernard Cartwright was hanged for the double murder. And . . .
5. Jack Medlock suspected, if not at the time then certainly

later, that Bernard Cartwright was not responsible for the murders.

Out of my own need for clarification of this final contradiction I resolved to take the approach that the reader will share over the next few chapters. I began what I suppose can only be described as a 'dramatic reconstruction' of the story, much in the manner of the true-crime television programmes I had seen over the years. As I began to assemble the story, I was able to add new pieces to help solve the mystery as and when I stumbled upon them during my investigation. I now know why Jack Medlock doubted Bernard's confession. I now know, also, that Medlock – and I had suspected otherwise at the outset – managed to remain true to his own conscience as well as to the constraints of his Square Dealer oath. However, before I could embark on this new course, I needed one more trip, to one of my oldest and most favourite haunts – the archive library of the *Weatherfield Gazette*.

The old *Gazette* building could do with a good clean these days. Alf, the steward at the door, is still there after forty-three years and I'm sure some of you will have come across him at one time or another, unfailingly polite and calculatedly miserable as he is, in a way that very few can make charming yet Alf still seems to manage it. The archive is no longer open to the public as most of the old paper copy has been translated onto computer disc and moved to the Public Library. The rest, we are promised, will follow as it is processed but it would be in here that I would be able to unearth any hidden gems from the mountainous and musty stacks that are the true heart of the day-to-day history of Weatherfield.

I still have a few strings left to pull at the *Gazette* and before too long I was burrowing through piles of dry and yellowing newsprint in the little side cupboard that has always been laughably referred to as the reading room.

There are no windows in this little sanctuary and the walls are decorated with a rich and subtly variegated patina of nicotine, accumulated from long years of either the intense search for knowledge or, more likely, the quiet escape from actual work. I love this room, mainly because there is nothing to distract from the endless possibilities that might lie within the innocent-looking pages of *Gazettes* long-forgotten. I especially love the fine, upstanding optimism of the old advertisements, those sketchily illustrated, ideal ladies and gentlemen only too proud and pleased to be the recipient of a pair Gastridge's Patent All-Weather Overshoes or a fresh tin of Eucryl, The Smokers' Toothpaste. Echoes, once more, of a bygone age. It was back to a time even earlier that I searched, however. I was looking for anything the *Gazette* might have had to say in the days between the arrest and the trial and then between the trial and the execution. Although I unearthed little more from any further account of the doings of Jack Medlock, I found far more than I'd bargained for in an unexpected place.

The Coroner under whose purview the Weatherfield district fell was a man by the name of James Campbell Hadfield, a Fellow of the Royal College of Surgeons and a man of considerable talents in a number of fields. He was, according to daughter Martha, a close friend of Medlock's in later years and the two men spent many a contented hour together after their respective retirements, reliving and elaborating their past adventures while debating the quality of Jack's supply of Single Malt. During his testimony, Hadfield had declared the cause of death in Alice Cartwright's case, in as close as he could get to layman's terms, to be '*a fatal head injury resulting from a depressed fracture of the cranium in the region above and to the outside of the left eye, consistent with a blow from a heavy, solid and sharp-edged implement, possibly a poker or similar such object.*'

This 'object' was never recovered. In fact, it never even

became an issue during the trial. Bernard said he'd thrown it away after the incident as he'd wandered the streets of Weatherfield in a daze of shock and remorse. Nobody pressed him on the issue. Under cross- examination, Bernard stated, 'Yes, a poker. I just picked it up. I was in a rage. It was the first thing I laid my hand on.'

A poker, then. The Cartwrights must have had a collection because a police photograph of the murder scene shows a poker and tongs set undisturbed by the fireplace. Also, it seems rather odd that a man who had just committed a murder should wander out of his house into the street, still holding the gore-smeared murder weapon and then proceed to carry it around Weatherfield with him looking for somewhere to throw it.

There is also a photograph of Bernard, posing proudly on the shop floor of Cartwright's, pointing out some aspect of the machinery to visiting dignitaries of the town. He is holding a clip-board in his right hand and pointing with the pen in his left. Knowing the point of impact of the blow that killed Alice, it seems unlikely that it was inflicted by a left-handed person, no matter how big or strong. If I could work that much out from this distant remove of over a hundred years, surely it would have occurred to two such sharp and experienced men as Medlock and Hadfield?

Hadfield had been an acquaintance of Jack Medlock's on and off for a number of years as their career paths crossed over the cooling remains of the unfortunate victims of violent crime. There is an interesting passage in Jack's memoirs; an account of an illegal boxing meeting in a barn on the outskirts of Weatherfield.

Illegal bare-knuckles contests were the subject of mixed views within the Weatherfield corridors of civic power. On the one hand they were condemned as a barbaric spectacle, unfit to muddy the civilized face of a modern enlightened community, while on the other, many felt that they were a means of keeping a restless male population from doing damage to one another or the community at large. The contests kept a lot of highly energetic young men quiet and sated an apparent need for violent spectacle that was better spent watching two hardened professionals go at it than in a confrontation with bottles and clogs in the centre of town on a Friday night. There is an account in Winterbottom's *Outlaws of the Old North-West* that describes a famous tussle between The Game Chicken of County Meath and Sailor John Barton, local man. The bout, fought in a Salford field and watched by a crowd of nearly 5000, lasted an astonishing forty-nine rounds before Barton retired.

Jack Medlock recalls a similar bout, the outcome of which caused some concern as one of the contestants appeared to have been subjected to a particularly savage beating. Out of a rather belated concern, Jack had spoken afterwards with the man's 'handler' and been reassured that no permanent damage was done. Indeed the man expected to be literally fighting fit in no time after the expert ministrations of a personage referred to only as the Doc. Medlock goes on to tell us that the pugilist's confederate then pointed out a distinguished, portly gentleman who appeared somewhat out of place among the sweating press of gamblers, spectators and sundry low-life. Medlock went to speak to the 'Doc' and, in the course of their conversation, both confided that they were simply there for 'research purposes' and their reputations would both be better served if neither mentioned the other's presence in politer circles.

Their research led them, apparently, to encounter one another on countless occasions after that. Jack never reveals the man's name, only that he held a position of prominence and great respect within his profession and that he had been fortunate enough to benefit from the man's experience more than once in a more official capacity connected with police work. Of course, James Campbell Hadfield figures significantly in the Medlock writings but he and the nameless 'Doc' are never linked. Surely they were one and the same man. A faded newspaper photograph of Hadfield shows us an over-weight, slightly bemused looking gentleman; an image that belies what must have been a far tougher and more worldly interior.

And so the two men knew each other, the two men closest to presenting a case either in Bernard's favour or to his detri-

Coroner, surgeong (and aficionado of the illegal fight game)
Doctor James Campbell Hadfield

ment. Both clearly had a renegade streak and both were familiar with the value of discretion.

I stated earlier that Hadfield had been a man of many talents. As I combed edition after edition of the *Weatherfield Gazette*, I came across a fascinating entry. I had gone back to the old index card system in the archive in search of Hadfield references, and found a pointer to a piece written in April, 1957. Thinking this was strange, I dug out the relevant piece from one of the endless boxed reels of micro-film that serve little other purpose these days than to gather dust efficiently. The article was one of those typical of local newspapers throughout the country. It bore the title 'Sixty Years Ago This Week' and was accompanied by similar excavations from ten and twenty-five years, the former on ration-book fraud and the latter on the shifting politics of Central Europe. I wondered why there was no fifty. Perhaps that week in 1907 was particularly news free but that did not concern me for long as I went on to discover another key piece in the puzzle. I include a section of the article below:

Sixty Years Ago this Week – Brutal Murder in Weatherfield. A Coroner's Report.

James Campbell Hadfield, the eminent local surgeon and police coroner today released the body of Alice Cartwright for burial. Mrs Cartwright was one of the two victims of the recent brutal slaying perpetrated by her husband, the wealthy mill owner and one-time philanthropist, Bernard Cartwright. The case has shocked the entire community. Apart from the tragic aspect of the deaths of a young mother and a popular local man thought by some to have been romantically linked to Mrs Cartwright, many in

Weatherfield now fear for the future of Cartwright's Mill and the jobs it provides. We have reported the progress of the trial of Bernard Cartwright in some detail in these pages but we can now also confirm, after a statement from Professor Hadfield, that the police officer in charge of the case, Detective Inspector Jack Medlock, conducted a lengthy interview with the accused, after the date for the execution was set and the authorities are now clear on the details of the crime and the motivation of the murderer who took the lives of his wife and her friend in a fit of jealous fury.

Nowhere, in police records, trial reports, Medlock's book or *Gazette* archives could I find any other reference whatsoever to this lengthy 'interview' that seemed to wrap up the affair in the eyes of the authorities. I found this astonishing. The journalist who compiled the retrospective feature adds some notes of his own at the end of the article.

James Campbell Hadfield not only enjoyed a notable career in surgery and forensics, in later years he experienced a number of remarkable adventures. Indeed, Hadfield was one of the few survivors of the tragic maiden voyage of the *Titanic*. He went on to work in the Far East for a time, helping to develop vaccines for a number of previously incurable tropical diseases and in his twilight years, this remarkable man even turned his hand to the writing of lurid, thriller novels under the pseudonym of Maxwell Kane. He claimed to have based his sensational plots for the likes of *The Torn Petticoat*, *Dark Passions* and *A Corpse in the Cupboard* on the events of the real life crimes on which he had worked for so many years.

Happily, it turns out that Weatherfield Library still holds copies of all the literary outpourings of Maxwell Kane. The nature of their contents is amply conveyed by the illustrated dust jackets, dating, as they do, from an era when the depic-

The Cartwright Murders

tion of a distressed but pneumatic young woman in imminent danger and strategically torn clothing was guaranteed to move a few extra copies. I borrowed the lot. Some proved to be worth little more than a quick gloss through, although the writer's authority in passages on the subject of anatomical detail was to be greatly admired. One title proved to be more interesting.

Murder At The Mill was Maxwell Kane's last work. He died shortly after its publication. The story itself is interesting enough but the true gold lies in the author's own introduction.

> *The events depicted in this story are based on a real-life criminal case. I am indebted once again to my dear, departed friend J.M. who held the secret for so long.*

I read through the night to finish the 'novel'. All the missing pieces were there. The following day I collated all my information; everything I knew or suspected, facts and conjecture from then and now. I decided to tell the story as Hadfield/Kane had done, except that I had no wish to sensationalize, exaggerate or hide the identities of the characters who inhabit the drama. What now follows is my own recreation of the Cartwright affair, written in the form of a fiction, if you will. Perhaps, inspired by the efforts of Mr James Campbell Hadfield, I felt the need to be free from the dry constraints of more day-to-day local history. Whatever the justification, I believe that, based on the evidence, what you are about to read contains the most likely interpretation of these tragic events.

PART 2

All the events depicted in the following pages owe their origins to references gleaned from contemporary accounts, police and court records and the writings of those involved or their associates. The dialogue uses the actual words reported wherever possible. Elsewhere, I have made a genuine effort, when using direct speech, to convey, as far I can ascertain, the character of the speaker or the spirit of the moment.

BOXING DAY

Christmas was over. The thin veil of snow, sparkling in the freezing, early morning half-light, lent the cobbled streets of Weatherfield a festive, almost romantic air that morning. The lamplighter, smothering off the streetlights and rapping on upstairs windows as he passed from terrace to slow-waking terrace, called out the dawn of another working day. Soon the identical, two-up-two-down rows; Kitchener Street, Tile Street, Wright Street and Nelson Street, would be alive with the clatter of clogs and the steam of breath rising over reluctant factory workers as they headed for the long day's grind at The Baron, The Empire or any one of the looming cotton mills that brought jobs – and, for a few, prosperity – to this grim, sprawling workhouse of a town.

Tommy Sykes hadn't seen his drinking mate, Nat Bardsley, since Christmas Eve and he cursed the biting cold as he waited for him, as on every other work morning, on the corner of Cartwright Street. As he stood, stamping away the chill, Tommy smiled, reflecting on their Christmas Eve revels. They'd had a skinful then, allright. Nat had promised to meet Tommy in the Tripedressers Arms at half-past seven. He'd been well over an hour late. Nat was a rogue, everyone knew that. He'd probably got a woman in. Tommy couldn't help smiling. Half the women at Cartwright's were after him and he'd probably already had the other half. Still, it was nearly nine and Nat was never one to miss his night out with a mate. Just as Tommy had been about to set off in search of his pal, Nat had appeared, somewhat flushed, Tommy remembered, but his usual hale and hearty self. He'd got a round in for everybody within earshot and soon the festivities were well underway. Tommy had thought no more of it at the time. This morning, though, thirty-six hours later, he was still trying to shake off the after-effects and Nat, true to form, was late again.

It wasn't yet fully light but it was getting dangerously close to being late for clocking in, Tommy would recall later, as he abandoned his wind-swept post on the corner and trudged off into the cold dawn, along Cartwright Street, to Nat's front door. Nat lived alone above a butcher's shop. Tommy hammered away at the glass and called through the letterbox. No reply. He rubbed a sheen of ice from the window with his coat sleeve so as to peer inside. There appeared to be a light burning on the landing. Tommy stamped off through the ginnel alongside the shop and into the back alley. He opened the gate into the back yard and called out again. Still nothing. Tommy was surprised to discover that Nat's back door was off the latch. He was also surprised by the sweet, sickly smell that hit him as he let himself into the kitchen. He was even more surprised to find his friend, Nat Bardsley, sitting in what seemed at first like an attitude of peaceful contemplation half-way up the stairs. Nat may just have been reflecting on the terrible nature of the gaping, sliced wound to the throat that had all but severed his handsome head.

Tommy's first instinct had been to sprint the short distance to Weatherfield Central Police Station.

Minutes later, as the growing bustle, rousing itself slowly to the bluff greeting-calls of neighbour and workmate, surged on down the street, a big man in a heavy, dark work-coat moved in the opposite direction. Hat pulled low, he slipped quietly into the side alley at the end of Cartwright Street, leaving behind the flow of bodies that headed on to the gates of the great mill that bore that same name. In the half-light, nobody noticed the expensive, highly-polished shoes and the sharp trouser-cuffs below the old coat's hem. The man kept his hands thrust deep inside his pockets – well away from the cold, it must have seemed. The man knew that only this way, could he hide the dark crusting of blood that still clung on beneath and around his fingernails and half-way up the sleeve of a crisp, starched shirt – grisly evidence of the horrific scene enacted close by, only hours before.

A Wedding

Alice Rafferty was getting married. Three o'clock. The women had finally managed to eject their bluff, edgy menfolk – crammed into collars for once – to the pub on the corner for a pre-nuptial pint. Just the one, mind. Grateful to be out from 'under feet', the men could cheerily revile the dreaded institution that they accepted would ensnare them all one day, if it hadn't already.

Not that the house was any more peaceful for that. Mary, Alice's mother and the acknowledged ruler of the Rafferty clan, was trying to direct the business in hand with all the success of a Keystone Cop directing traffic. Alice could only laugh in the midst of the chaos but then you rarely saw Alice without a smile on her face. Now she had all the more reason. She'd never been so happy; for herself, for her family and for the life she was about to embark upon with Bernard, her serious, almost comically noble man whose overtures she had accepted without a second thought. That was three months earlier on, of all places, the roof of Bernard's factory, the mighty Cartwright Cotton, as the two of them had surveyed the smoke-blackened Weatherfield skyline and imagined it their own story-book kingdom.

Alice stood now before the full-length mirror. She was a real beauty and no mistake; and though she'd never say it herself – others did that for her regularly enough – she knew it. Even if it hadn't been for the curling half-smile and the cheeky gleam in her eye, she'd still have turned heads wherever she went.

Alice Cartwright, with mother Mary, on her eighteenth birthday.

Those two extra weapons just made the whole thing unfair.

Yet nobody had a bad word for Alice, save, perhaps the occasional wife who'd had to tug her gawping husband's ear back to the matter at hand long after Alice had sauntered past. She had a wicked sense of humour and wasn't afraid to air it at her own expense. Though never well off – just the opposite, in fact, until now – she was generous, straightforward and could swear like an aggrieved sailor. All of which attributes, though immunity was impossible, armed her against the hardships of everyday working life in the carding-room at Cartwright's. She was one of the girls. And now she was marrying the boss.

At the other side of the Weatherfield tracks, in a rather better-appointed upstairs room of a somewhat grander house, Bernard Cartwright was wrestling with his tie, damn it. And where's the ring? If anyone needed a drink today, it was Bernard. Who's got the ring? For the umpteenth time, the best man, old schoolfriend Albert Cox, wearily confirmed the secure presence of the wedding band in the watch-pocket of his suit. Just don't lose it.

Bernard Cartwright, cotton magnate, hard-headed business baron, lord and master of a sizeable wedge of all he surveyed, had been transformed into a panic-stricken wreck. Albert thought this hilarious and the more he showed it, the more edgy Bernard became.

They were ready. In truth, they'd been ready for an hour but Bernard liked to make sure. Albert knew how nervous his friend must be. Eyebrows had been raised in some of the more genteel drawing rooms of Weatherfield when it was announced that the mill owner was betrothed to an Irish girl from the carding room. Honestly, dear, how does it look? The first wife's not been dead that long, surely, poor woman. And those two young boys . . .

It was hardly the behaviour expected of such a prominent public figure.

If Bernard Cartwright was aware of the whispers he could not have cared less. He was in love with Alice. She loved him, he was sure, and she loved the boys. Little William and Robert. They were Elisabeth's sons but Alice loved them. Bernard knew it. And if they didn't hurry up they'd be late for the church.

Albert smiled and, in spite of himself, traced the ring-shaped bulge in his watch-pocket one more time, just to make sure.

The ceremony was a grand and wondrous thing. Tears were shed, admiring gasps were uttered at the first sight of the bride and the vows, according to the unwritten rule of such matters, were stumbled over in the groom's determination to get them right.

The church was packed. Well-wishers who hadn't made the guest list nevertheless thronged the churchyard. Everyone agreed Alice and Bernard made a fine couple. The couple's way to the waiting carriage was showered with a coloured rain of rice and confetti. Women glowed for Alice and for women and weddings everywhere, while the men shook their heads and smiled for Bernard, the lucky so-and-so. And, as is always the way, some, who knew neither bride nor groom, gave it six months. It was every wedding Weatherfield had ever seen, only bigger.

Those six months passed. Then nine. No doubt, to the disappointment of many, the Cartwrights were still as happy now as on their wedding day. Alice had given up her place among the ranks of women in the carding room so as to better look after Bernard's two young sons. Beryl Baines, the boys' governess of recent years, had been relieved of her duties. Bernard had thought her slightly stiff but civilized departure a painless one but Alice had known otherwise.

On 26 July 1897, Alice gave birth to Amelia; red hair, blue eyes (which later turned green) and certainly nothing lacking in lung-power. Seven pounds one ounce. Thankfully – apart from a hint of her father's jaw-line – the image of her mother. Bernard was the proudest man on earth and marked the day, despite his wife's protestations, with an announcement and presentation of the new-born baby girl to his entire assembled work-force, necessitating a full fifteen minutes celebratory suspension of all Cartwright's operations. A birth is one thing but business is business.

*

The factory, like the family, was thriving. The couple were happy, wealthy and set fair for the coming new century in their very own gilded cocoon of good fortune.

The Cartwrights lived in a grand house overlooking the one green oasis at the heart of Weatherfield. On a weekend, the park was alive with promenaders, footballers, kite-flyers, courting couples, miners practising 'peggy' – their exclusive stick-and-missile game – for another local 'World Championship', and in amongst it all, the Cartwrights would while away the time playing with their children and, like reluctant royalty, acknowledging the greetings of passers-by.

Did Bernard think Alice would ever go back to work? What would she want to do that for?

Bernard Cartwright at thirty-five. Murderer?

When all the children are in school. She couldn't see herself rattling round that big house all day. Not unless they got rid of the maids so she'd at least have something to do.

Bernard laughed. She never need work another day in her life. Surely Alice realized that. He hauled himself to his feet and began to marshal the boys for a game of catch. Alice smiled up at her husband fondly, knowing that this good and loving man would never understand what she meant.

A Football Match

Park Villa could always turn out a good side. One of the two or three best in Weatherfield and it was about time they started damn well proving it.

Nat Bardsley fingered the oddly-shaped, good-luck talisman around his neck as Billy, the manager, launched into his customary pre-match exhortation to great deeds of athleticism. Yes, Billy. You're right, Billy. It was more than the majority of the lads could do to shrug off the slow-dragging effects of a gallon and a half of bitter the night before. Still, this was a cup match, a one-off. Villa were as good as any on their day and better than most; better than George Street Youth, for sure, who, in Nat's eyes and those of his team-mates, were little more than a bunch of prancing, college-boy poseurs who'd better have packed an extra set of shin-pads if they were expecting to clock-in for their soft, so-called jobs on Monday morning.

Villa were pit lads, mostly, with a handful from Cartwright's. Hard lads. But they could play, all right. The trouble was, they could also drink. If Park Villa had been teetotallers, they reassured themselves regularly, neither Preston North End, Bolton Wanderers nor Blackburn Rovers would so much as get a look in. Still – more mutual reassurance – if you worked as hard as they did all day, you were entitled to enjoy yourself on a weekend. After all, we're harming nobody apart from us-selves, lads.

The Cartwright Murders

Tommy Sykes was Nat Bardsley's best mate. He was a full-back of limited skill but boundless stamina and he could tackle like a vengeful landslide. As the team walked from the changing-rooms down through the park to the pitches, Tommy dug up an old refrain for his mate's benefit.

When are you going to get out of that pit and come and work at Cartwright's? Nat, for his part, dusted off his habitual response. When they can offer me more brass than I'm on now for less graft than I'm already doing. Nat insisted Tommy couldn't argue with that but that didn't stop Tommy. What about the conditions, the muck? Do yourself a favour, man.

Villa won that day, 2-0. Nat Bardsley scored the first of the goals; a header from a corner. The following Monday, he lost two fingers of his left hand in a fall at the pit. The ceiling of a side-tunnel collapsed killing four of Nat's work-mates. Nat himself had been farther up the tunnel, away from the shaft, and was one of seventeen more exhausted, battered and filthy men, dug out after nearly eleven hours. With the injury to his hand and a badly-twisted right knee, Nat's football career would have to go on hold for the rest of the season. His life as a miner was over for good.

Two weeks later, on a fine late-spring day, Nat was limping along in the wake of his erstwhile team-mates in his new and self-appointed role as motivator-in-chief for the Cup run that had taken them to today's semi-final. Across the wide expanse of open land that stood between the park pavilions and the football pitches, Nat spotted a big man swinging two small, laughing boys high into the air, one after the other.

As a ten-year-old lad, the proud but overburdened Nat Bardsley had struggled along behind his dad, Frank, as the faithful carrier of the basket. The basket contained the birds and the birds contained the secret to a freedom and exultation of the soul that Nat was only just beginning to understand. With the release of a pigeon, high into the great grey yonder that they knew must be blue somewhere, the miners and cotton workers of Weatherfield would experience for a moment, however vicariously, that escape from earth-bound drudgery all of them dreamed of but none ever so much as remotely believed in for themselves. The pigeons flew for them and at the weekend meetings, the fanciers – cynical, unromantic men like Nat's dad – could exchange tales of exotic travels and glorious homecomings like weary adventurers from a more colourful world. It was at these meetings that Nat had learned the lore of the birds – the legends of the great, long-distance flyers, the tragedies, the fabulous secrets. He'd learned to spot a champion, to handle and reassure the warm, trembling thing that waited only to burst free from his hands in that wild, ragged flurry that magically turned to grace once the earth was forgotten. It was at these meetings that he'd envied the older boys, entrusted with their own birds, mixing with the men as equals and speaking their special language.

One of those favoured boys, he remembered, was a big, quiet lad who always came on his own carrying a smart wicker and leather basket alive with blue-grey beauty. Now he was standing breathless before him, over twenty years later. Nat had always known the name of the mill boss – everyone did – but he'd never put it to this familiar face from the past. To Nat, the smiling, red-faced man in shirt-sleeves, this prince of Weatherfield in an unguarded moment of simple pleasure, was just big, quiet Bernard, the rich lad who knew about pigeons.

The two of them talked briefly. No, Bernard hadn't been able to keep up his hobby. Too much work.

Shame, they agreed. What was he up to these days? Really? Bloody hell . . . oops . . . sorry, lads.

And so on for a minute or two. Bad luck about the pit. Aye, well. Thanks.

Then the pause that meant the reunion was over. 'Appen Bernard could go up and have a look at Nat's pigeon coop one of these days, away among the 'pens' on the edge of town? Be like old times.

No slaves to the decorum of their elders, the boys demanded more madness.

Thanks for the offer. Bernard swung back into his fatherly duty. Happen he would.

For the next few weeks, Nat would hail Bernard as a long-lost pal whenever he saw him in the park. He'd joke that it was about time Bernard gave him a job up at the factory. Bernard liked the lad's spirit. And there was, as it turned out, a fair chance of a suitable job coming up. He said nothing but knew in his own mind the seed was planted. Nat might just make a half-decent addition to the Cartwright's work force. He was popular, fit despite the injury and obviously wasn't frightened of a hard day's graft, coming as he did from the back-breaking labour he'd sustained for the past fifteen years or so. And on their brief passing acquaintance so far, when Nat had been the consistent model of politeness, Alice seemed to like him. She was generally a good judge.

The Mill

Alice brought baby Amelia into work, all wrapped in her fine, soft white woollens, for the factory girls to make a gurgling, precious fuss over. Their general attitude to babies, Alice knew, was that every one they'd already suffered was a curse while every new one to arrive was a blessed miracle. Each was the most beautiful child ever and this one was no different from the rest – though better dressed.

As all within earshot laughed and swapped stories in a happy, unforeseen break from cotton, up above, from the window of his office, Bernard Cartwright looked down from his papers and smiled on the twin, immovable pillars of his perfect life – his family and his work.

The girls ribbed Alice for the charmed life she'd come to know, the fun she'd missed, the scandal she'd have loved to have been around for. Would you believe it? That Peggy Dobbs off Tile Street. Again. Talk about common? Needs a new string for her drawers, that one, and no mistake. And Alice laughed the way she'd always used to. She missed all this but couldn't say it, while at the same time her once-intimate circle was gnawed by an unwonted envy that none would show. Alice was a pal. Still. Always would be. Good luck to her. The shadow of awkwardness that crept over them after only a few short minutes of reacquaintance was thankfully dispelled by the presence of the children. Amelia and the two boys, William and Robert – aren't they shooting up like weeds, the pair of them – gave everyone a renewed focus once they'd run out of things to say to form a temporary bridge between the two worlds – that of the boss's wife, primrose path before her, and of the threadbare-pinnied 'shoddy' hand whose future consists of wondering whether her husband will come home drunk or sober.

Nat Bardsley didn't see Alice as he approached, all fake bluster, in his mission to get the girls' minds back on doing some work.

Are we bothering, girls, or are we just having a chat, as usual?

Oh. Sorry, Mrs Cartwright.

Alice almost smiled and dismissed the slip but kept it back for wickedness and for her friends' sake.

The girls rejoiced at seeing cocksure Nat colour up and look nervous for a change. Not that they didn't like him; they did. It was just that he always seemed to get 'too much of his own road'.

Alice did smile now as the gathering dissolved. Alice, who'd never be seen as mean-spirited by anyone, man or woman. No bother. She was just taking the children up to see their Dad.

Honestly, I didn't see you. Sorry.

I said, no bother.

She went on her way across the factory floor. Nat watched her go – his eyes lingering a second too long for the liking of the women on the conveyors. A voice called out, rich with triumph, 'That bloody shut you up for a change, gobby.'

Nat didn't catch it. Alice rounded a machine, boys running along in tow. The moment was gone. The women jeered and Nat rallied, to resume his role as Cartwright's invulnerable jack-the-lad.

If you lot ever got any work done I might not have to come round and sort you out so often.

Take more than you to sort us out, lad. This followed by a burst of earthy speculation. Everything back to normal. Almost.

Nat waved away the banter as he swept off down the line of machines. God, she was beautiful.

Upstairs, Bernard was busy but then Bernard was always busy. Below the office, the unfathomable, beehive surge of work went on as it always did, and presumably always would. Meanwhile, Robert might need glasses. William had a tooth loose – see Dad, this one, it wiggles – and Amelia looked like she was getting a cold. And now, Bernard would be late home. A meeting. Sorry.

Alice stared out across the work space as her husband told her something about a difficulty getting some ship or other unloaded in Liverpool. Bills of something or other. Cash flow.

Out there, submerged now by the eternal roar of mill noise, the girls rocked suddenly away from their stations, as one, in a silent explosion of laughter at some wise-crack, then returned to work, pointing, gesturing, shaking their heads. Alice was lucky, they'd said earlier, as they'd said on that first day when she'd told them how Bernard had asked to take her out, and as they'd said again on her wedding day. And every other day. Lucky. As everybody said. Everybody, all the time, told her how lucky she was. Alice had a caring, generous husband who would drag the stars down from the sky for her if she only asked; three fine, healthy children and the kind of magnificent house she'd only read of in books about another kind of people. She loved them all. Yes, she was lucky.

And still, out there, the great belly of the factory churned, on and on.

A hundred yards from the window, lost in the sea of machinery, Nat Bardsley wrestled to free a wooden bobbin that had become trapped in a twisted mesh of wire. It was a struggle but he'd get it cleared if it took all damned week. Determined it wouldn't beat him, he focused his mind on that one single act and away – though he would have fought any man to deny it – from the insistent and perfectly-formed image of Alice Cartwright that had altogether invaded his brain.

Sunday in the Park

There was a band. Once a fortnight throughout the summer and on into the cooler autumn evenings, the burgundy-uniformed Empire and Cooperative Brass Band of Weatherfield would assemble in the little blue and gold stand by the park lake. There they would run through their customary assortment of hymn tunes, waltzes, marches and sundry classical interpretations best avoided by brass instruments. Jim Hadfield would join them. He liked to fall asleep in the deckchairs the council so thoughtfully provided. He liked to get out of the house and let his wife and three daughters restore order after Sunday lunch without his interference. He did not like brass band music but that was a minor consideration, especially as on most Sundays he was accustomed to chance upon someone who did and was even now reclining, eyes closed in reverent appreciation of what was, to Jim's ear at least, a rather raucous cornet in the act of murdering Mozart.

Jack Medlock opened one eye as his friend dropped into an adjacent rain-bleached deck chair of the kind only a Weatherfield park could sustain.

'Ssshh!'

Jim had no intention of interrupting. He'd have needed a cannon. A minute more and the piece was over. The tough-looking little man whose attention had just been so captivated, sat up and committed himself entirely to Jim's presence.

'Sandwich.'

It was more an opening gambit than a question but that was always the way with Jack. He assumed the answer before he'd asked the question and so rarely bothered to leave space for the opinion of others. It was a part of the copper in him. Jack often said that if he sat here long enough, every villain in Weatherfield would stop by out of curiosity and end up staying to give him enough informa-tion to keep the station busy for a month. Jim suspected that this was somewhere close to the literal truth as Jack surely couldn't be that drawn to Strauss and Sousa, could he? It wasn't natural. Still, it wasn't a question he'd ever dared put.

Jim took the sandwich and the two men ate for a while in silence. They had an odd way between them for friends. They hardly bothered with greetings as it was generally obvious to one that the other had arrived in the same place, so if they'd anything useful to say, they may as well just get on with it. And so, they did.

Jim was first. 'Called off next week, I believe.'

'So I hear.'

'I'm told this Jarvis feller has got a cut over his eye "as won't heal itself up proper".'

'Not all his medical contacts are as good as yourself, then, obviously.'

From the way it was delivered, Jim wasn't sure if this was a compliment to his own skills as a surgeon or merely a criticism of the profession in general. Jack managed a half-smile, possibly to confirm the former. Jim was never sure.

Jack Medlock and Jim Hadfield shared all kinds of professional concerns in their respective positions as police inspector and county coroner though they rarely discussed work on their own time when they could debate a subject of far more interest to both – boxing. Sadly, their mutual passion was one that shared with the two men themselves the position of being of considerable importance to the law. This was bare-knuckle boxing. Raw, brutal fighting. Organized, big-business, hugely popular and strictly illegal. The 'sport' had been outlawed way back but Jack Medlock was drawn to it as a door into the underworld – or at least that's what he would have told himself. As for Jim, he'd been awoken one night years ago by a gambling acquaintance bearing a large, half-dressed and badly-battered gentleman in tow. Jim had provided stitches and potions wherever necessary – pretty much everywhere as it turned out – and within this round, unassuming and otherwise strictly law-abiding man there was born a dark fascination that had grown and that he could now share with another.

The two men had met in a dimly-lit barn, over an unconscious pugilist, had recognized one another instantly and, in seeing the necessity for mutual confidence, formed a friendship that brought them together usually in the event of some violence or other but occasionally in more peaceful settings, today being one such. So long as, Jim told himself, you could manage to ignore the band.

'And business in general?' Jim enquired.

It seemed almost more than Jack Medlock could do to summon a weary response. 'I'm sure that as we speak, somewhere in Weatherfield, some considerate soul is making work for me and thereby trouble for somebody else. No doubt Monday morning will reveal it.'

Jim took the hint. 'Then we shouldn't let it spoil what's left of Sunday.'

But Jack was suddenly taken by the theme. He sat upright. 'See that woman?'

Jim turned to follow the direction of his friend's gaze. Across the open field was a woman in her twenties, sitting on a bench and rocking a fine, coach-built pram with one hand. Even at this distance, Jim could see she was lovely. His medical eye discerned a fine bone-structure beneath the loosely-gathered, long red hair.

'Well?'

'What's she doing?'

Jim shrugged. 'Rocking her baby's pram. Sitting.'

Jack leaned back in his deck chair and closed his eyes again.

'You make a better doctor than you would a copper,' he said.

Jim Hadfield looked at the woman again and saw nothing new.

Jack remained the image of casual detachment. 'Chap fifty yards away? Her left. Dark-haired feller about thirty.'

Jim looked. There was indeed a young man of that description leaning against the fence and facing towards the band stand, seemingly lost in rapt attention to the music.

'So?'

'She's married, we assume.'

'I would hope so.'

'But not to him, you'd imagine.'

Jim replied that so much was obvious as he had yet to see any connection between the two people whatsoever and demanded to know why Jack Medlock did.

'Just a sense,' came the reply. 'Not that it's a crime but . . . like I say . . . trouble for somebody sooner or later. Another sandwich.'

Jack could not have known that the trouble would, in fact, come to his own door before too much longer. He had another, vaguer sense that he might have seen the man before. Maybe at a fight. A football match, perhaps. Nevertheless, as the band struck up 'The Blue Danube', such considerations were forgotten while, at his side, Jim Hadfield could see that the subject was now closed.

Across the park, Alice Cartwright rocked Amelia into a deep, smiling sleep. Bernard had taken the boys up onto the Edge, the high outcrop of moorland that pushed out from Weatherfield and marched on up, windswept and barren, into the Pennines. He loved to sit up there, above the grime, and gaze out over the town through the clearer air. Now the boys were of an age, Bernard was determined they should learn to appreciate this simple joy for themselves.

In taking Amelia for a stroll in the fresh air herself, Alice was now wondering whether the baby's welfare had been her prime consideration. Or had she known, deep down, that she might catch a glimpse of her husband's works foreman among the many Sunday promenaders. Either way, it had happened. He'd spotted her in passing – though she'd had to pass twice – and nodded a polite greeting. Merely polite. She'd made sure he saw her stop and sit, a momentary and innocent repose. Mother and baby on a park-bench. What could be more natural?

Nat Bardsley had also stopped, staying well within Alice's sight, not fifty yards away, so that, idly – just in the natural course of things, you understand – he might occasionally glance back in her direction then be all too quick to look abashed when their eyes met – accidentally, of course – for the briefest of moments.

It was an elaborate and dangerous game. The wheel was spinning now and both Alice and Nat, though they may have seen themselves watching it from above, were held captive in its centre.

Nat, too, had taken the chance on an unforeseen encounter. So far, no more than an exchange of pleasantries

Weatherfield Park (now the 'Red Rec'), showing the bandstand
and pavilion in the 1890s.

had ever passed between them. Surely an enquiry after the
baby's health could not be seen as inappropriate?
Something, anything, that would look like a reason to speak
when both he and Alice – Nat was sure it was both of them –
were so wishing it.

Nat dived and was instantly over his head.

'Fine day, I reckon.'

The fifty yards to reach her had seemed as many miles but
Nat had somehow negotiated them, his heart bursting and
his stomach churning with a dread he'd never felt before
around any woman until now.

'Let's hope it keeps up.' She was mortified. A more articulate voice in her head mocked at her puny effort. Is that the
best you can do? Alice was desperate to keep the blood from
her cheeks. A hot pause seemed to stretch until . . .

'Family all right, are they?' Nat shifted his weight from one
foot to the other in the asking and discovered he now
weighed 500 pounds.

'Grand, thanks.' Again Alice's inner tormentor stabbed
her. Grand?

'I'll be off, then.' And so he was, rescuing them both. Nat fled, as slowly as he could manage, hot now, terrified and stupid with elation.

Meanwhile, on the park-bench, another part of Alice Cartwright, a part that wouldn't speak of it for fear, knew that her charmed life would never be the same again.

Meetings

They met when they could. Nat lived in two rooms above a butcher's shop in Cartwright Street and it was there they first made love, urgent, guilty and wonderful.

There was always something; Alice couldn't get away, Nat was working, Bernard wanted all the family to go to Southport to see his mother, Nat's father was bad with his lungs. Everything seemed to conspire against them.

For Alice, this whirlwind transition from good wife to adulteress had brought about a state of near-shock that she carried with her always and, she was convinced, barely managed to hide. Guilt and confusion became her constant companions. She loved Bernard. She loved her children. Yet she also loved Nat with a wild panic she could neither control nor deny. She felt as if every nerve-ending in her body was alternately stone dead or more alive and electric than she'd ever known.

Alice hated this cold, shabby betrayal and knew she could neither justify it nor end it.

Nat was a dreamer. He had a thousand answers for every question yet never one that would prove practical. The only thing he knew for certain was that he'd never experienced this urgent sense of vitality before, this need. He'd always been in control. And there had been plenty of women, that was for sure. Married, too, some of them. He'd never let that worry him in the past. This was different. The thought of Alice going to another man's bed every night ate into him, especially at work, where Bernard would pass with some comment or question – rarely an order, that wasn't the boss's way – and Nat would feel himself instantly transformed into some slimy thing that he could not but loathe. Time. Things would work out. It had hardly been a few months since that first magical, clumsy encounter in the park. Time would see to it.

There was no time. It had to be now and always. Where? That was easy enough, although God only knew how nobody had yet seen her coming and going. When? It was always 'soon' and yet never soon enough.

Tommy Sykes prodded his mate in the ribs with a discarded bobbin. 'Where the 'ell have you been, then?'

'You what?' Nat shook himself back into the cacophonous realm of cotton.

'You were miles away, man. And apart from that, I thought we were meant to be having a pint after Sunday dinner.'

'I weren't so well.'

'Couple o' pints would've sorted you out, then, I reckon.'

Nat and Tommy were best mates but at that moment, Nat wished Tommy would disappear for ever and leave him well alone.

'Have you seen that new 'un in th'offices?'

From Tommy's tone, Nat could tell that the woman in question – it was always women with Tommy if it wasn't football or beer – must have already created a stir among the male half of the work-force.

'Annie summat-or-other. Fit as a butcher's dog. Knows it, an' all.'

Normally Nat would have responded with more enthusiasm and he could tell that Tommy was disappointed when the lurid anatomical analysis that followed was not met with greater appreciation.

'Wait 'til you see her, man, that's all. You'll be slavverin' same as rest of us, just you watch.'

Nat acknowledged that this would no doubt be the case and changed the subject to one of speculation as to what the new season might hold for Park Villa. They'd started well over the first few games and Nat was back to full fitness. Thus Tommy was soon launched out far into his vision of unstoppable sporting feats for their team and Nat was happy to let him sail away.

The room above the butcher's was cold. It was always cold.

'Tell him, then.' Nat was sitting at the foot of the bed. How many times had they been through this?

'I've told you, it'd kill him if he found out.' Alice dressed herself in the half-light through the drawn curtain.

'It's killing me, as it is.'

Alice left off her buttons for a moment and came to sit beside Nat. His eyes pleaded with her, not so much – though Nat himself was unaware of it – for her to go out and confront Bernard with their joint betrayal, as for the strength to watch her leave once again and then survive until their next encounter. Nat wasn't stupid. He knew what she faced. Equally, he knew that she was stronger than he was and if either of them acted to force a way beyond their present circumstance – this half-life of hastily snatched and secret minutes in shadowy corners – it would be Alice and not himself.

Nat begged his own conscience to tell him he wasn't a coward but it never quite seemed to manage it and so he hated himself all the more for his inability to act.

And now she was leaving.

Alice had been gone two hours. The baby had slept throughout, in her carrying-basket at the foot of the bed, not five feet away, while the mother had been so desperate for her own stifled cries not to wake it. Now the two of them were home and the house had never seemed so empty. Bernard would be back soon from his weekly meeting with the other power brokers of Weatherfield. Doing whatever it was they did. They normally finished around eight and it was a good twenty-minute walk from the Lodge. What did they get up to in there, those sober, comically serious men with their rigid convictions of what was right for all and sundry? Alice had smiled at Bernard's assertion of quiet gatherings around good works and philanthropic ambition. She suspected more that they just liked to play God.

And then he was home, swinging the boys in before him, having picked them up from a favourite treat – pancakes at their Auntie Iris's – and shrugging the cold off along with his big, black overcoat. The one he always wore, though he could have afforded twenty new ones that Alice insisted would have better reflected his status as a great man of the town. But no. Good, kind Bernard. He kissed her now, a gentle brush of familiarity before shepherding the boys upstairs to the bathroom.

She had a bathroom, Alice thought to herself, suddenly and for no good reason. No Rafferty had ever had a bathroom before. Then she thought of that fleeting half-kiss and what had gone before, then of her child, still sleeping and the shouting boys upstairs and how her loyal and loving husband had no idea. And how the magnificence of then fought so bitterly against the shame of now.

Late October. It was already dark through the factory windows by the time Nat Bardsley got round to locking up and found Annie Collier waiting for him, hard-eyed and silent on a bench just outside the offices. He thought everybody had gone home. She knew they had.

Nat hadn't really wanted to, but he soon forgot all that as she pressed him up tight against the factory wall. They'd flirted briefly over the last few weeks, in the way that everyone in the place flirted. Certainly with the now famous Annie.

Annie was a teaser, they all knew; she enjoyed the banter with the lads and the outrage of the other women.

And now it had come to this. Nat was rocked, first by the urgent heat of her desire for him, then by the coldness with which she went about fulfilling it.

It was all over quickly and Nat was still fumbling with belt and buttons when Annie left him, offering no more discussion on the matter than she had when she'd found him.

Nat carried on locking up. Reeling. Stunned by what had just happened, as if he'd had no part in it. Just get locked up, Nat. What else was he supposed to do?

The next day at work Tommy Sykes noticed, in the odd way such things have of hanging in the air for an age, the glancing, split-second eye contact that passed between Annie and Nat – hers of triumph, his of panic. It was there and gone in an instant but Tommy stored it. That Nat; he was a lad, all right.

It was around this time that Bernard Cartwright began to sense that his wife might be unwell.

Christmas

Snow in Weatherfield. It usually waited until January for the real, hard-biting frost that marked the long, grey winters in this part of the world but in the run-up to Christmas the temperature had gradually dropped and the clouds turned that shade of swollen, steel-blue that all those who woke to it, scraping the ice from the inside of upstairs windows, knew signalled a heavy snow-fall. They were soon proved right. Two days before Christmas Eve 1897, the streets and pitched roofs around Cartwright's were wreathed in a hand's depth of sharp snow. It had fallen white but it lay a dirty, pale grey, followed down throughout the next day by the fine settling of factory grime that did the job regularly, not just on the odd winter outing.

It would be a notoriously cruel winter that year, not just in Weatherfield. The sharp teeth of the cold had already begun to bite deep. Still, the worst was to come.

Inside Cartwright's mill, away from the cold, away indeed from the machines but still cocooned within their droning din, Nat Bardsley insisted once again, in an urgent whisper that he wished could be a scream, that he wasn't interested in Annie Collier.

She blazed, her face inches from his own. He was interested before, wasn't he?

Nat replayed the only line he had for her. That was once. It was a mistake.

Annie demanded to know what was so wrong with her. Other men would kill for what he'd had for nothing. And he'd enjoyed it, that much he couldn't deny. See. See the colour in his face. She knew it. Her husband meant nothing to her; he was a pig. A word from Nat, just a word, and she'd leave him to his drink and his fags and his racing and his damned, black cough.

Her fingers dug deep into Nat's arm. He twisted free and walked away back into the heart of the mill. What had he done? He knew what he'd done; it was what he'd always done and most shaming of all, what he'd probably do again if some more-than-willing other, as hungry and as brazen as Annie Collier, pinned him up against a wall as she'd done a few weeks earlier.

He'd escaped for now. A group of women passed him, preventing Annie from following but he knew the overtures would begin again and he only had himself to blame. Why hadn't he just . . . but it was too late now. A man called out to come and have a look at this machine. Nat, his mind reeling inside the crazy whirlwind of all he'd released, had never needed the distraction of work as much.

Above in his office, Bernard Cartwright could not help thinking that Alice had looked pale that morning as she had on so many days lately. She seemed distant. He'd asked her about it. Was she not sleeping properly, kept tending to the baby in the night? Should he get the doctor in? But Alice had waved away his concerns, gently as always, insisting she was fine. He loved her for that. Always more troubled by what the children might be going through, or Bernard himself.

They needed to get away, that's what it was. As soon as he was able, Bernard told himself, he would take the whole family somewhere healthy; somewhere he'd read about. Switzerland, perhaps. That was where the fancy people went, wasn't it. Then that's where they'd go – Bernard, his wife and their three children. Settled, then.

But when? There was always so much to organize. And so, with his mind back on his work, the master of Cartwright's returned to the safety of the world he knew best.

Alice met Nettie McVie on the market on the day before Christmas Eve. Nettie had nipped out to get her vegetables for Christmas dinner before her shift started. Stan had got a goose in already, a big one off a bloke up at the pens. Should keep the kids quiet. Not as big as the one Alice'd be cutting into, though, she teased. Lucky so-and-so.

Nettie had worked opposite Alice on the belt. They'd laughed, moaned and gossiped together from the first moment that Alice had started the job. Nettie had been there ten years already then and she'd taken to the newcomer as though she were family. Alice missed her desperately.

So what was the latest from work?

The two shared an awkward moment over news of a recent pay appeal that had been turned down – worker and boss's wife – but shook it off for friendship's sake. There was always their Christmas Box from work, Nettie offered by way of covering the cracks. Always grateful for that.

And Peggy Banks was having another. What was that, now, nine? How did she feed them all? What does she feed her husband on, more like.

Frances's mam had died. Friday. It had been coming a good while, mind. And Tommy Sykes had got the backside of his overalls stuck in a machine and they'd had to cut him out with scissors. Nettie said it was better than a pay rise seeing him waddling off across the factory floor trying to cover his bare arse with his hankie. He'd never live it down.

And that tart Annie Collier from the offices. Chasing Nat Bardsley now, they reckon. Caught him, an' all, by all accounts. Wouldn't be surprised.

Nettie looked up to see the church clock beyond the roofs of the market stalls. She'd better be getting going. Work, and all that.

All the best, love. Come and see us, won't you. Merry Christmas.

Alice Cartwright did not hear the greengrocer ask her if there was anything she wanted.

Christmas Eve. It was dark out. Snowing. In an upstairs room, a young, single man was drying his going-out shirt in front of a coal fire and trying not to scorch it again.

Nat Bardsley knew that in spite of his aching need to see Alice, this was not a time to push. She had her family to attend to; her children came first.

As quickly as that thought entered Nat's mind, he tried to banish it for it meant something so hard and clear to him that he dared not even contemplate it. Perhaps Alice couldn't admit it to herself – didn't even realize it – that her children, along with the life she now enjoyed, would always come first. It was the gnawing doubt that wouldn't go away. Always perhaps this and perhaps that. What did he have, after all, to offer a woman who'd grown used to all manner of comfort and finery, as, surely, Alice had done? Certainly not a wage from Cartwright's if the truth were revealed.

As he washed away the working day's grime with a wet cloth, over the sink in his small room, Nat's thoughts flew in every direction, always taking Alice with them. America,

Australia, anywhere. They were both young enough, strong enough.

Then he'd crash back to earth, grounded by that same nagging thought that just wouldn't stay out of his head – Christmas, the children come first. And next Christmas? What then? What about next birthday, next sniffling cold day, school-day? And so it became every day and Nat sank into even deeper despair. He needed the threatened gallon of bitter alongside his boozing pal, Tommy; the noise of a bright, smoky tap-room, men's raucous, unthreatening banter and the promise of a stupid, drunken sleep well into tomorrow. Christmas Day. On his own. Christmas Day.

And suddenly, as he attached his collar in front of the old, black-blemished mirror, the picture of Alice with her children was forming before him once again.

He'd thought to have seen her at the end of the day, coming – in the authorized version – to meet her husband and then walk him home through the snow-covered park. A caring wife's nod to Christmas. But she had not come. He had not been able to bring home with him that look from her that would have sustained him over this day or two at most, this lifetime, of not seeing her.

Nat pulled on his jacket, cap and white, silk scarf, closed the door behind him and marched out to meet Tommy in The Tripedressers Arms at the end of the street, where he intended to get blessedly, disgustingly and unfathomably drunk. This he managed with a degree of enthusiasm that was a surprise even to Tommy.

On Christmas morning at the Cartwright house, after the joyful frenzy of present opening orchestrated by the two boys, the sun came out on a fine, cold day. From their bedroom window the boys thrilled to the prospect that the snow would stay with them for a while yet. Alice looked out over the park and onto the near-deserted streets beyond. Families were just beginning to emerge into the white fields, wool-wrapped, trailing the dog, the new sledge, the shuffling over-bundled toddler. Soon, she knew, the park would be alive like those scenes from the Dutch paintings she'd marvelled at in a Manchester exhibition that Bernard had been invited to attend. She remembered how he'd been worried that it might bore her.

Bernard would want to take the boys out soon. Their excitement was already getting too big for the house. Alice would take Amelia to see her own family Christmas in a very different part of town. It would be crowded at home, as ever. Noisy and spontaneous. Warm and safe and simple. And she would go by Cartwright Street. Nettie's thrown away scrap of gossip corroded her every thought. She had to know.

Jack Medlock thought he'd never seen a finer Christmas morning. He had calls to make to parents, relatives, friends. This was just the way Jack liked it. He could visit, share the brief glow of others' celebrations for a while, then politely leave them to it, escaping into the perfect peace of the shimmering cold. His life was his own, and though he kept it well away from his work, it was marked by the same ordered and methodical stamp. The baffling complication that was 'other people' could be kept at arm's length for a time yet.

As he passed the bandstand in the park, drinking in the sharp air that today, at least, was not laden with the outpourings of factory chimneys, Jack was reminded that he must call in at Jim Hadfield's. The doctor would feign mortal offence should he ignore the invitation proffered so casually a few days earlier over a body recently dragged from the canal.

Shouts, away over the white field, stitched across now as it was with ragged lines of darker footprints, drew his attention to a man he recognized at once. The mill owner, Bernard Cartwright, trailing two boys and a giant, wooden sledge with real, steel runners. Probably out to give his wife a bit of peace.

The man was batting snow off his overcoat by the time Jack

reached the park gates. The boys had thought it the best fun in the world to push their father off the sledge into the snow as he, for his part, made an elaborate show of hogging their new toy for himself. Screaming with laughter, the two little lads now fled, away up a slope with their reclaimed sledge bouncing behind them.

Jack had seen Bernard, not that long ago, at a combined lodge meeting of the Weatherfield and District Square Dealers. The mill owner was somewhere way farther up the arcane scale of importance the Order maintained. Jack could never remember all the rigmarole. He turned up at meetings and stuck by the principles of the thing. That was the important bit. Which reminded him, he was late with his subs – something else that would have to wait.

Jack pressed on, away from the park and towards the centre of town. Jim had promised a particularly rare malt to toast the festive season; not the kind of thing Jack could generally manage for himself on a copper's wages. Maybe he was in the wrong job.

Alice hesitated before putting the brake on the baby's pram outside the butcher's window on Cartwright Street. It was broad daylight. To risk knocking on the door was to state publicly an interest in the doings of the single upstairs resident, Nat Bardsley. She had no doubt that more than one curtain along the street would have twitched already. Alice knew that the neighbours around here never missed an opportunity for the magical processing of even the tiniest speck of gleaned information from rough conjecture into pure certainty. This was the life-blood of these streets – other people's business.

Let them talk.

Alice knocked. Finally, the door was opened by a bleary-looking Nat, his elation curbed by near-panic at her lack of discretion, ushering her into the white-tiled shop interior that seemed barely warmer than the streets outside.

What the hell was she playing at?

An image of family life from the Dickens pamphlet,
Weatherfield Days.

Her silence, her searching plea deep into his eyes, though
it could have only lasted a few seconds, stopped Nat in his
tracks. He knew something was wrong. He sensed in that brief
second what it might be and stood there, dumb and swaying
in the middle of the butcher's floor, like a stunned bullock.

Alice managed to free the only words she could find. 'I
want to know.'

'What are you talking about?' Nat was near to vomiting
with dread.

'You and Annie Collier. I want to know.'

Nat couldn't move. Her eyes wouldn't let him. Part of him almost began to try and change the subject, as if it were nothing really and she'd forget if only he could make her laugh, or cry, or something.

'Once. We did it once. It were nothing. She damn near raped me, Alice, what were I supposed to do?'

Her look in return, though it did not mirror her heart, seemed almost one of pity. 'When?'

'How d'you mean, when?'

'Before us or after us?'

And now Nat had the means by which to save himself, or damn himself. If only his bursting brain could decide which was which.

'Before.'

It was done. Too late to change. Alice seemed to shrink a little and Nat took the chance, stepping forward to risk a tentative embrace. He'd saved them, surely. She backed away, her eyes glazed now, distant, not meeting his.

'I can't stop,' Alice said. 'Folk'll be talking already. I . . .' She was even now backing the pram and her sleeping child out through the front door.

'It were before, Alice, I swear it were. Honestly. You know I love you. Alice, come on . . .'

'Do you?' She was in the street now and Nat knew he could say no more. She had flown from his hands and was away.

The nosy old bat opposite had picked just this time to put her milk-bottles out, damn her.

Alice looked back once, confused, drowning and desperate for the will to say something that would work, that would let her hold him now and never have to think or feel ever again.

All that surfaced was a smile that broke his heart, then, 'Merry Christmas,' as she walked away.

As Alice rounded the corner of Cartwright Street and the pale, hollow shade of Nat Bardsley faded back into the butcher's shop, on the other side of the street a stocky figure in flat cap and long overcoat ground the stub of a cigarette into the snow, turned and walked away.

Bernard Cartwright had an annual ritual that he had never failed to observe since the year he took over the day-to-day running of the factory from his father. He would go alone into work on Christmas Day, when the vast bank of machines lay still and dreaming like a dragon asleep on its golden hoard, and drink a toast in celebration of the day and of his own, many blessings.

Bernard had always felt himself the luckiest man alive, even before he'd met Alice. Now he was sure of it.

He could picture her at home now, marshalling the children, laying the table, having dismissed all help. She'd come home earlier from her family's house with a fierce determination to have everything 'right'. There was still half of Christmas to go and they should make the most of it, all five of them, together.

He'd offered to give the factory a miss but Alice had insisted. It was his thing and he should keep it. It was a part of who he was and he must never change.

Bernard had smiled at her intensity but he'd been proud as he picked his way along the streets through the now dimming light of the afternoon. The lamp-lighter would be out soon. Some things would carry on, Christmas day or not, and Bernard was glad of it.

Inside the factory, he leaned against the frame of a machine and surveyed the cavernous realm that spread out before him. It was as magnificent in repose as it was in the full display of deafening power that was every other day of its existence.

The other man called out from across the shop-floor. Bernard had heard the footsteps of someone coming through the building. He'd assumed it might be a passing constable or one of his watchmen checking on an overlooked side-door.

He was surprised to see a stocky man in his mid-thirties, not one of his own workers, Bernard knew, crossing the floor to meet him.

'Can I help you?'

'I can 'appen help you more.' The man's wheezing voice and the wracking cough that followed marked him for a miner. The brown dimp between his fingers couldn't have helped his condition.

'I were thinking of calling at your house but with it being Christmas I reckoned it could wait. Then I seen you out so I thought, why not . . .'

Bernard took an instant dislike to the man's supercilious tone, to say nothing of his uninvited presence.

'You'd better say what you've come for and clear off or I'll sling you out myself, lad. I don't even know who you are, for a start.'

'No but I know who you are, mister high-and-mighty Bernard Cartwright. I know yer missis, an' all.'

Bernard moved towards the man, who took a step back and lifted a hand.

'Hold yer horses, eh. I were out on me own business, in first place but I thought I might as well do us both a favour. You know, with it being Christmas, like.' The man smiled and Bernard hated him for it.

'Before you chuck me out I thought I'd just let you know about your missis calling in on Nat Bardsley at that butchers on Cartwright Street earlier on.'

Bernard reeled. 'What?'

''Appen she were only after a bit o' meat. There's plenty others go for t'same.'

Bernard lunged at the man but he was already running out through the banks of silent machines, laughing as he went. Bernard shook with anger and with something else far deeper and more terrifying to him.

The man was a lunatic, surely, a trouble-causer, drunk for certain. Bernard leaned back against the frame and saw, try as he might to suppress it, the image of the pale and distant Alice that had so troubled him of late.

When Bernard Cartwright returned home later that evening, as the gas lamps outside lent the frozen streets a soft, blue glow, he found his wife sitting on the floor of the parlour, reading a story to the enraptured children in the shadow of the great Christmas tree he'd dragged home from the market a week before. That was in another lifetime.

She looked up and smiled as he hung up his old overcoat.
'Alice?'
'Mm?' She lowered the book and raised her perfect face to look at him.
'Are you happy?'
Alice laughed at the ridiculous notion that she might be otherwise. Scattering the two boys with the promise of a resumption of the story before bed, she rose and ushered Bernard towards the dining-room and the supper she'd prepared for them both.

He was lost. Bernard allowed himself to be led, unable to speak then in the certainty that if he could find any good words at all, tears would surely betray them.

Weatherfield, April 2000

The old bandstand on the Red Rec should have been pulled down long ago. It's an eyesore now; a sad, broken-down apology for the proud and brightly-painted little confection it must have been in Bernard Cartwright's day.

Late in the month, the snow came again to Weatherfield. I'd planned to go and watch the opening day of the Central Lancashire League cricket season so I should have been expecting it. Instead, I found myself en route from the *Gazette* buildings, sitting in the crumbling, wind-swept alcove that made up the last shelter the little bandstand could provide, wondering who Shazz and Dobber might be and how they'd managed to get hold of so many different colours of paint. I'd sat here before as a young man, courted girlfriends here, even heard a band play once, in the time of the annual Carnival, long since abandoned as we're told 'people don't want that kind of thing any more'. They clearly want this instead.

And from the Carnival days I went further back, prompted by the weight of books and papers in the briefcase under my arm. As I watched the snow fall and disappear across the black surface of the lake, I pictured Bernard and his two small sons, rolling and slithering down the hill to my right, not far from the house, that still stands, where Alice Cartwright's life would soon come to such a violent end. I thought I could see, too, the solitary shade of Jack Medlock, watching in the distance but as he approached he transformed into the more familiar figure of Denis, the park-keeper, skewering crisp bags and hiding inside his Walkman.

I reflected on all I'd read and learned from source after source that had opened up to my research and on how much Jack Medlock had actually told James Campbell Hadfield of the minutiae of the Cartwright Case. Was there something he'd left out? I was beginning to think so but this was too cold and forlorn a place to stay and ponder it.

I left the bandstand and pushed on through the biting wind into what remained of the story.

Murder

The record book at Weatherfield Central Police Station – always kept so meticulously, he would often remind his superiors, by Sergeant Fred Platt – had only one reported incident for Christmas Night 1897. That was the noisy arrival of a young woman nursing a cut lip and the early development of a black eye. The woman's name was Annie Collier. Through her angry tears, she recounted how her husband, George, had rolled in stinking drunk, ranting and threatening even worse violence before inflicting the blows that caused these wounds so clearly visible on her face. It wasn't the first time. She'd had enough and she wanted him damn well charged and locked up. That's if anyone could find the drunken pig. He'd stormed out, raging into the night. That was around one, she said, and he'd not been back since, thank God. She offered only the hope that he froze to death.

Bernard Cartwright woke around four on the morning of Boxing Day. He was alone in bed. Alice had gone into the baby's room sometime earlier to quiet Amelia's growing restlessness and had yet to return. She'd probably, as on so many previous occasions, fallen back into sleep with the child in her arms. Bernard had come upon the pair of them in just such a dreaming bundle countless times as he'd risen for work over the months since the child was born. It had always filled his heart to see them so and he wished for that comfort again now as he crept across the dark landing.

The baby slept soundly in her cot. Alice was not there.

He checked the boys' room, then all over the house, calling her name softly. Only then did Bernard Cartwright don his overcoat and go out into the freezing night, praying that the children would not wake in the time it would take him to cross the half mile to Cartwright Street.

Bernard ran where the ground would allow. It was icy underfoot and more than once he fell, bruising his hip and grazing his hands. The seven or eight minutes it took to cross the town seemed more like hours. He stopped for breath at the corner of Tile Street, only yards from the butcher's door, wondering, now he was finally here, what he would do.

It would look ridiculous, surely, the boss standing at his foreman's door in the early hours, demanding his wife return home with him that instant. If indeed she was there at all.

Bernard peered in through the glass. There was a dim light

in the area he knew must be around the foot of the stairs. The back way might reveal more and at least any confrontation would be partly hidden away among the yards and out-buildings.

The back door was open. Bernard went through the tiny backyard, slithering once on the frozen cobbles before managing to steady himself by grasping the frost-coated handle of the back door.

What met him beyond the door was a scene that turned his soul to ice for the rest of his days.

In the pale light of the butcher's back room, Bernard saw Alice, sitting on the floor at the foot of the stairs. She was moaning softly, staring into the depths of a dark pool that spread out before her across the stone floor. He knew instantly, though he could discern no colour, that it was blood she sat in. In those first panicked seconds he thought the blood must be her own. Her coat was thick with it and one of her hands stood out dark against the tiled wall, a trailing smear marking the path of her slide to the floor.

Then as he went to her, he saw that the blood was not hers. He saw the other seated figure on the stairs, covered in blood – his foreman, Nat Bardsley, dead and staring out with a strangely questioning look and a deep gash opened wide across his throat. Bernard could see, too, a line of scratch marks down Nat's cheek. A woman's hand. Oh, Alice, how could any heartache, no matter how cruel, come to an end as useless and as pathetic as this?

Alice was murmuring, moaning incoherently, then suddenly she seemed aware of her husband's presence for the first time and tried to push herself to her feet like a child caught in the middle of a prank, wiping the stain from her coat. He went to steady her and only then did he see in Alice's hand the heavy steel meat-cleaver, still black with Nat Bardsley's blood. Bernard had to prise her icy fingers open to release it from her fist.

Alice was in a trance, gripped by a stupor of shock and horror the like of which Bernard had neither seen nor had any notion how to deal with. He picked her up and carried her from the house, through the back door and out into the night. He carried her the half mile through the backs and ginnels of Weatherfield until they reached their home and he could set her down on a chair in the kitchen and try to help her to speak.

What had they done, all of them, to bring about this horror, this evil? Bernard in his panic and confusion could only see one thing. His wife had gone to her lover – had he betrayed her with another woman just as Alice had betrayed Bernard? The nasty little sneak in the factory had hinted at it – and in a jealous madness she had picked up the cleaver from the butcher's bench and swung at the man. Had he struck her? Attacked her? If only Alice would speak to him.

Suddenly she looked him straight in the eyes. The expression on her pitifully drawn face shocked and terrified him. She screamed. On and on. He begged her to stop and tried to hold her but she fought him with a strength he'd never have believed she could possess. He tried to calm her but she scratched and kicked at him, snarling and spitting out words that had no form or meaning. Her breath came in harsh, ragged sobs as she whirled away through the kitchen, snatching herself free from his desperate efforts to hold her. Bernard managed to fasten onto a flailing arm then saw in the corner of his eye, her free hand reach out, clawing madly across the surface of the table. His instinct told him to release her and sway back as something sharp gleamed dully through the air in front of his face. Alice's furious, wild momentum pitched her forward. She slipped. There was a sickening, soft thud as she dropped to the floor. Then silence but for the sound of Bernard sucking in what little air he could into lungs that felt like fists clenched tight.

His panting breath clouded like steam in the half-light of

Jack Medlock demonstrates the hard-eyed stare that struck
fear into the Weatherfield criminal classes.

the kitchen as Bernard bent to lift Alice back to her seat and
to restore her to herself.

Alice stared at him but Bernard knew that those eyes that
could once say so much only told him now that she was
dead. The dull, sunken blush at the side of her head showed
the place where she had struck the corner of the heavy oak
table in her fall. Bernard laid her gently now on that same
table and as he did so, he noted the first spreading colour of
morning begin to suffuse the heavy night sky over the park.

He washed his hands carefully, quietly now, and went
upstairs to wake the boys.

*

Beryl Baines hadn't seen her old employer over the Christmas period. A shame, she'd thought. She still loved those children even though her place as their guardian and protector had gone to the cocky little Irish girl from the factory. Still, none of her business that, now. She certainly did not expect to see Bernard Cartwright at half past five on Boxing Day morning with both William and Robert at his side and a bundle in his arms that could only be the baby Amelia. But there he certainly was, standing on her front door step with a face as white as a sheet and a voice just the wrong side of calm.

Bernard said he was sorry. Very polite.

She reassured him. Too worried to ask. Of course it was no bother.

Beryl Baines ushered the little boys in and took the baby from Bernard's arms. He thanked her and left. Just like that. No word of when he'd be back. Beryl took the children, lit a lamp and went to the pantry to see if there was enough left in at least to give the poor, shivering little things a drop of hot milk.

Through the ice that was forming in his brain, Bernard Cartwright saw what he must do. He went next to the yard at the back of the mill and the bays where the wagons loaded. He swept up a tarpaulin cover that had been keeping a pile of coke dry by the trap-doors to the great boiler rooms, folded it under his arm and walked once again down through the back alleys to the butcher's shop and the body of Nat Bardsley that he knew would still be sitting on the stairs, waiting for him to return.

It was no more than four hundred yards from Cartwright's to Nat's lodging but this was the second time in as many hours that Bernard had carried such a burden through the streets. He was exhausted. Only an automatic, numbing instinct to put one foot in front of the other – one more time until he made it – got him through the factory's back doors, down the steps and into the boiler room where the great furnaces glowed softly, waiting to be fed and restored to the raging intensity that would heat the factory through the coming day.

There was nobody in sight. Bernard knew the inner workings of the great beast well enough to be certain that he would remain undisturbed for another half hour yet.

He opened the heavy furnace doors and fed the lifeless body of Nat Bardsley into the searing, liquid heat.

The blood-slick tarpaulin followed before Bernard dropped the bar back across the cast-iron door and left the cellars to emerge into the first true light of the morning.

By the time he reached the butcher's yard once again, Bernard had dropped the bloody cleaver off a bridge into the canal and his mind was forming the strategy that he must now adopt. First, though, the back room, the dreadful, bloody scene of the accident – for surely she'd not meant this – must be cleared of any trace of Alice's presence.

Bernard stopped as he reached the back door. Something was different, altered, and for those first few seconds, he couldn't see what it was. Then it struck him. Someone else had been there. The bloodied footmarks across the backyard now told of other visitors since he'd found Alice. Alice who now lay dead on her own kitchen table.

He'd done what he could. She was gone from here. The body of Nat was gone. Now he must be gone too. Someone would certainly be back any minute, looking around for Nat, maybe for Bernard himself. He couldn't stay here a second longer. If there had been other signs of Alice being there – a bag, a scarf – surely he would have seen them. Anyway, what did it matter? Nat was dead and nobody would find either him or the marks on his face that pointed to Alice as the killer. And now he, Bernard Cartwright, had killed Alice.

Still, the course Bernard now set out for himself, showing clear above the churning chaos of his thoughts, would see a kind of order restored. If madness can be born in a moment, it was then that it truly emerged in the mind of Bernard Cartwright.

Tommy and Jack

'Just slow down, eh, Mister Sykes? If he's as dead as you reckon, he'll not be going anywhere, will he.'

First thing on a Boxing Day morning and Jack Medlock was stuck with this.

Tommy Sykes scuttled ahead, his clogs rattling on the glistening cobbles as Jack Medlock and his muttering constable followed in his wake. Tommy had damn near crashed the police station doors off their hinges not much more than quarter of an hour earlier, with a tale of blood and horror that had even the weary desk sergeant raising an eyebrow.

One for you, I think, Jack. As so it proved.

They arrived, breathless now, at the back gate of Middleton's Butcher's, reached through a dingy ginnel that led into the alley behind Cartwright Street. Jack was beginning to regret the extra whiskies Jim Hadfield had plied him with the day before. And the bottle he'd gratefully taken home to keep him company last night.

They paused before crossing the yard and the constable stepped aside to let Jack take the lead.

'Can't think of a better place for it, meself. Keep fresh in this, an' all,' he whispered, out of Tommy's hearing, as the Inspector passed.

'Can I recommend that you avoid thinking wherever possible, Constable Burrows.' Jack wasn't one for the gallows mentality that his men liked to arm themselves with in defence against the nastiness they faced on a daily basis. He understood it but it wasn't for him. The constable looked suitably chastened. Idiot, Jack thought. 'Shall we go inside?'

*

Jack looked long and hard into the ashen face of Tommy Sykes. He didn't look or sound like a liar or a crank but then, Jack Medlock met all sorts in a day's work, some of them a damn sight weirder than this one.

Jack surveyed the scene before him, taking in every detail, careful to keep himself and his two less cautious companions to the edge of the room and out of the sticky puddle on the tiles. There were footprints across the floor.

'Well . . . it's a butcher's and there's blood. Nowt special so far.'

'Burrows!'

'Sorry, sir. I'll shut up, sir.'

'Do.'

Jack turned to the baffled-looking Tommy Sykes.

'You wouldn't wind me up, would you, Tommy.' It wasn't a question.

'Honestly, Mister Medlock, it's hardly the kind o' thing I'd make up about me own best mate, is it.'

'I suppose not.' It would certainly rank as a pretty sick joke. Still . . .

Jack dismissed the thought. The trembling, confused little man at his side did not convey the impression of a good actor trying to keep a joke going.

'Tell me again what you saw.' Jack never took his eyes away from the gory spectacle inside the room, meticulously recording every nuance.

'It were Nat, honestly, he were just sitting there. I only come 'cos I thought he were going to be late for work.' Tommy stared into the puddle and shuddered.

'Describe him.'

'He were dead.'

Jack's delicately raised eyebrow signalled to Tommy that this information was now superfluous and further detail was required from this point on.

*

An hour later, Jack had the area sealed from prying public eyes and entrusted to the care of a worthy sergeant. Tommy had been plied with hot, sweet tea and had given Jack everything the Inspector could have hoped for under the circumstances and perhaps, Jack suspected, a little more besides.

Tommy Sykes seemed to think the relatives (apart from the parents, both now deceased) had all gone to America years ago. Nevertheless, it was time to inform whatever family Nat Bardsley still possessed of his untimely demise. Sadly, even Tommy could only speculate that, besides Nat's mates, his boss Bernard Cartwright was just about the only other person who might be interested in his foreman's death. Him, and about a hundred women who would now be obliged to chase someone else.

Jack decided, on reflection, that it might be easier to start with Bernard Cartwright.

The mill owner was not in his office. This was rare, the secretary told Jack, as the inspector folded the Cartwright home address into his watch-pocket. As he emerged back onto the shop floor, a woman's scream cut through even the ear-splitting clamour of the machines. Workers on all sides stopped what they were about and looked up from their stations. Jack could sense the swell of rumour, building from the one fact he was sure was at its heart and rising to course like a wave through the men and women now turned towards himself and the uniformed constable at his side.

'Go and find out who that was, constable, if you don't mind. Meet me outside.'

In the yard, Jack Medlock pondered the question; if Nat Bardsley were as popular with the ladies as his mate Tommy had suggested, then how many of the working men of Cartwright's would be all that sorry to see him dead?

The constable emerged from the building at the same time

as a woman of around fifty bundled two small boys and a well-wrapped baby through the open gates into the yard, skirting past a heavy-laden, horse-drawn cart as she did so.

Sometimes Jack Medlock could forget a face in seconds, especially if there were sufficient, expedient reason to do so. More often though, he was cursed by an inability to prevent just about every face he ever saw from entering the steel-trap filing system of his brain where most would remain undisturbed for ever more. These two boys rang a tiny, Christmas bell in Jack Medlock's head. These were Bernard Cartwright's sons. The boys from the park.

Jack headed the woman off before she reached the main doors. The perfect gentleman with the easy smile.

'Come to see their dad, have they?'

'Come to find him, more like. He drops them on me in middle o' night, then I don't see hide nor hair of 'im.' Beryl Baines was struggling to retain her dignity . . . 'Not that I mind like' . . . so much so that she neglected to ask what business it was of this nosy stranger's in the first place.

'Have you not tried taking them home?'

She gave him a look of pure disdain that confirmed her years as the most conscientious of family servants.

'D'you think I'd be dragging them out here if there'd been any answer?'

Jack acknowledged the point. It was only then that Beryl took in the presence of the uniformed constable. Her eyes narrowed.

'What's going on?'

Jack was in the act of composing a working response when he was distracted by his constable, whose head was turned towards the roof of the factory. The man's pointing finger rose slowly to track the direction of his gaze. 'Mr Medlock? There's a bloke up there just standing.'

Jack turned. He was sure there would be plenty of reasons for any number of men to be up on Cartwright's roof at all times of the day and for all kinds of reasons. Nevertheless, he followed his constable's pointing finger.

A portrait of Alice on the occasion of her twenty-first birthday.

Bernard Cartwright was standing on the raised wall at the very edge of the factory roof. His dark shape was etched in sharp silhouette against the pale grey morning. Almost as if he'd been listening to them, Bernard turned his head and looked down at the little group in the yard. His eyes met Jack

Medlock's and held them for a moment, as if trying to pass on a message. Then he turned, almost imperceptibly, to look at the children. A second later, he was gone.

Jack Medlock was already half-way across the yard when he turned back to the constable and barked out the order to go and get more men, fast. As he reached the door he stopped and turned again as though angry with himself.

'Get the children inside where it's warm.' Then he, too, was gone. Beryl Baines was sure she'd never come across such a rude little man.

Jack realized pretty quickly that if Bernard Cartwright wanted to lose him in the bewildering maze of the factory he would have little difficulty. The mill owner could probably disappear for weeks into the vast belly of his personal tame beast. Yet there he was, fifty yards distant and standing in full view.

'Mr Cartwright. Do you mind if we . . . ?'

Jack didn't reach the end of the question, shouted as it was over the din. Bernard Cartwright turned, seemingly unhurried, and disappeared from view amid a sea of cotton bails and machinery.

The policeman set off at a run. Heads turned but the life of the factory seemed little perturbed by this small drama unfolding in its midst. By the time Jack reached the end of the narrow lane formed by the banks of carding machines, Bernard had disappeared yet again.

'Did you see where he went?' Jack snapped the question out to a man in oily overalls who looked up languidly.

'Who's that then, lad?'

'Your boss, man. Did you see which way he went?'

''E's generally up in t'office. You're going wrong road.'

The affable worker was in the act of pointing Jack's way but the policeman was already moving quickly away through the rows of machines and scanning the spaces between, left and right. At the end of the aisle he stopped and shook his head. This was a waste of time. He realized that his search had, in any case, brought him back to the area overlooked by Bernard's office.

The little room from which Bernard Cartwright controlled his empire was reached by an open staircase down which the secretary Jack had seen earlier was now picking her way, laden with a stack of papers and envelopes. Through the glass behind her, Jack thought he saw a dark flutter of movement, a coat perhaps, then nothing. He vaulted onto the stairs, shoving past the outraged secretary and scattering her burden like confetti before bursting into the office only to find it empty. The other exit – of course, how could he have not seen it the first time? – that led out onto a fire escape, had somehow been barred from the outside. Jack stood for a moment in front of the great, floor-length windows that invited the pale winter light to flood the room. His eyes searched the yard below. From directly beneath the window at which Jack Medlock now stood, the big dark figure of Bernard Cartwright suddenly appeared, as Jack knew it would, striding more purposefully now, not towards the main gates but out in the opposite direction towards a small side exit, half-hidden by bales and palettes in the corner of the yard. Five seconds later he was gone. All Jack could see now behind the high factory wall was the canal, cutting dead straight through the heart of Weatherfield and away into the world beyond. The way Bernard Cartwright was now headed.

Jack turned to leave the office. He needed his men now. Where the hell were they? The constable had better be back with reinforcements by the time he got down to the front gates or there'd be even more trouble. A lengthy late-night spell wandering the docks could soon be arranged.

As he passed the big oak desk at the centre of the room, Jack paused to pick up a hand-written note; small, neat and signed with the name of Bernard Cartwright.

'Sister will take the children. Could someone please go home and look after my Alice. I am very sorry.'

Jack Medlock slipped the note into his coat pocket and made his way out of the building through an aisle of silent, staring cotton-workers. Gathered together on the wet cobbles outside, his men were waiting for him. Jack called out to them the second he emerged into the cold, 'Come on! He's off up the canal.'

Even before all the men were through the door in the far wall and out onto the canal-side, Jack Medlock had detached two of them to go and find whatever awaited their arrival at the Cartwright house.

Seconds after the little knot of policemen had split up and disappeared, Beryl Baines bustled the children out into the yard once again. She had been confused and annoyed. Now she was beginning to worry.

The Canal

There was no sign of Bernard Cartwright along the stretch of the canal that Jack Medlock and his men now covered, half-running, half-walking, their clouding breath billowing above them in the cold morning air like steam over a train. The laboured wheezing of the heavier of the constables only added to the effect. Even the canal was feeling the weather as it, too, ran thick and slow alongside them like a polished iron girder. Then, as the hurrying group rounded the shallowest of bends, they spotted their man, maybe 300 yards ahead of them and moving at a fast walking pace that now broke into a shuffling trot.

The constable to Jack Medlock's right pierced the morning with a shrill blast on his whistle that made the inspector's head jerk away to one side as though he'd been slapped. Without slowing or turning to look at the man, Jack offered a gentle lesson in policing. 'Might I ask the purpose of deafening all and sundry within a mile radius, Whittaker? This is not a damn silly fox-hunt, man.'

The constable replied in solid and earnest fashion, 'Sir. Requesting the gentleman to stop as we are currently in pursuit, sir, and also alerting other members of the force as may be in the vicinity that the pursuit of a suspect is, in fact, taking place and that any assistance would be appreciated. Sir.'

All this without missing a stride on the uneven tow-path.

'I'd save my breath for running if I were you, lad. If he'd been looking to meet up with us for a chat, we wouldn't be doing this, would we. And if any of the lads on the beat do come running they can only get onto the canal from behind us. So . . .'

'Point taken, sir.'

They were visibly gaining on Bernard now and Jack and his whistling constable had pulled ahead of the two other men in the chasing group. Jack knew from his younger days, exploring here when it was strictly forbidden, that the canal would soon disappear into a tunnel. They would lose him in the dark and the countless side arches that led off to God only knew where. Beyond the tunnel came the point where the canal turned down through a weir and a series of locks that ran close to the railway line, and only a few yards away was the viaduct that crossed the Weatherfield valley and carried the lumbering goods trains across the Pennines to the weaving mills on the other side.

'I think he's trying to make for the viaduct. If he gets to the tunnel we'll not stop him.' Jack quickened his pace and, as if by some telepathic link, Bernard turned to look back at that same moment and quickened his own.

'Permission to run on, sir.' Constable Whittaker was already moving ahead. There was maybe a hundred yards between them now.

Ahead of them, Bernard Cartwright suddenly dipped across to the canalside, climbed a lock gate and leapt down onto the opposite bank. The drop below had not given him a second's pause. They were losing him.

'Go on, then. Hold him if you can. And be careful.'

Jack's breath was coming in ragged bursts now but the constable lengthened his stride into a sprint that soon began to close the distance between himself and their quarry. Whittaker reached the lock. Not as desperate as the man he chased, he wavered, wary of the danger as he balanced on the timber beam of the massive gate handle. Then he leapt and was over, running strong now and gaining fast.

Bernard, sensing the danger, dragged his big frame into a last, desperate attempt to reach the tunnel.

From half a football field away, as he picked his way over the drop into the lock, Jack Medlock was aware of the mouth of the canal tunnel grown wider ahead of him. He saw, too, the lunging shape of the constable grab and cling on to the legs of the fleeing man who stumbled now against the tow-path wall and tried to shake the smaller man off like a bear battling a baiting dog.

The two were still struggling and flapping in a dark tangle by the edge of the water when Jack Medlock, in a furious, charging bundle of absolute single purpose, crashed into Bernard Cartwright's chest and sent him reeling back against the stone arched entrance to the tunnel. The momentum of the collision took them away from the prone figure of Whittaker who lay struggling and winded now, behind them on the tow path.

Bernard's hands rose instinctively to protect himself and ward off his smaller assailant but Jack Medlock drew on instincts of his own, garnered in countless street scraps and from the close-quarter study of hard men who earned heavy purses from such matters. He struck Bernard a sharp blow just below the sternum that carried every remaining ounce of his energy and drove all the wind from the bigger man's lungs.

Bernard Cartwright shrank and slumped against the wall, fighting noisily for air as Jack Medlock tensed to strike again if need be. Whittaker was on his feet now, ready to join in and even up his own score a little.

In the melée, Bernard's head came up suddenly and he looked straight into Jack Medlock's narrowed eyes. His voice rasped out, harsh and desperate.

'Will you deal square with me, Jack?'

The spring that was coiled to propel the policeman into further action slackened in an instant. A flicker of astonishment flashed across Jack's eyes then was dispelled as if he'd been shaken from some brief distraction. Jack forced himself to restore an outward semblance of composure. Then, as if he'd suddenly remembered his purpose, Jack raised a hand to prevent the advance of Whittaker and the two lesser athletes who had now, finally, caught up with events.

He looked up into the face of the big, wheezing man whose collar he still gripped and slowly releasing it, took a step back. Jack's cold expression masked the angry confusion that was even now racing around his brain.

'Aye, I will.'

The words came out like a mantra. Words he'd said so many times in just the same level tone but never in such circumstances. Words that reassured a brother in the Order of Square Dealers that their encounter had moved onto a different plane of trust and intimacy. What was this man doing, this murder suspect – for surely his actions could have no other interpretation – invoking a code, an unbreakable bond, that Jack Medlock was duty-bound to observe? If he could.

Bernard nodded his head almost imperceptibly and blinked at the little group surrounding him as if he'd just woken from a sleep.

One of the constables now recovered from the rigours of the chase and keen to be of use, approached Bernard with handcuffs at the ready. He had barely opened the first clasp, the mill owner raising his hands meekly to accept the condition, before Jack Medlock surprised them all with the sharp impatience in his voice.

'We don't need that.'

The view towards Salford from the Weatherfield section
of the Bridgewater Canal, circa 1900.

The inspector seemed lost in his own thoughts as he turned without another word and began to stride back along the tow-path towards the comparative warmth of Weatherfield Central Police Station.

Bernard and Jack

Jack Medlock's sergeant, the thoroughly methodical Fred Platt, thought it downright irregular that his superior should want to spend time alone in a tiny cell with a probable murderer. Still, we all know what he's like, Fred reminded himself. If that's what the boss wants . . .

But as old Fred rummaged through the keys for the one that would open the cell now holding Bernard Cartwright, it became clear that any further encounter between the inspector and the suspect would have to wait.

One of the two men who'd been despatched to investigate the Cartwright home had returned breathless with the news that the body of a woman lay, as if carefully positioned in an image of peaceful repose, on the kitchen table of the house. The constable's colleague would remain on guard at the kitchen door to await the arrival of his superiors and Jack was informed that the two men had touched – I can definitely assure you of that, Mr Medlock, sir – absolutely nothing.

Alice Rafferty lay like the dreaming queen of a Pre-Raphaelite fantasy. Jack Medlock almost regretted that she had been obliged to linger still in this cold, stark kitchen instead of floating gently down the leafy, woodland stream that her pale dead beauty seemed to warrant.

His reverie was quickly banished by the more pressing needs of the murder investigation. It seemed clear enough that the woman had died from a heavy blow to the side of the skull. There was dried blood, plenty of it, yet it was not hers. There's our first little mystery, Jack thought. Something to discuss with Bernard, no doubt.

The coroner would sort all those details out when he got here. Had somebody alerted Mister Campbell Hadfield? It was all being taken care of. Sir.

Jack was more taken by something small and shiny on the floor by the black-leaded kitchen fireplace. It was not the kind of thing he could have identified himself – he'd never gone in for that kind of thing – but he knew someone who might at least tell him where it came from, if not how it got here.

Jack knew, for he'd given the instruction himself, that Tommy Sykes would still be somewhere about the station drinking tea and trying to pull himself around from his early morning shock. What was it the man had said? 'Some foreign letter-thing round his neck but nowt else as would've made him any different from any other bloke.' If only that were true.

Jack Medlock picked up the strange little medallion by the end of its broken chain and slipped it delicately into his pocket.

*

The machinery of murder was grinding into gear; the body of Alice Cartwright was on its way to the morgue, neighbours were inventing their own definitive versions of events and reporters were stirring from their slumbers, sniffing the air for sensation. Somewhere in a white-tiled room that reeked of disinfectant, Jim Hadfield would be raising a single, worldly eyebrow. Here we go again.

Meanwhile, Jack Medlock was back on Cartwright Street, inside Middleton's butcher's shop looking over the scene of a different crime.

Jack was now faced with the prospect of this other, far nastier business in its way, being part of the same series of events that had led to the locking up of one of Weatherfield's most respected citizens in an eight by six cage in the cellars of the town's main police station. He shook his head. What a mess this was turning out to be.

Sam Middleton was in a frenzy. To his discredit, this was born not from a sense of civic outrage or that an alternative form of carnage to the usual had taken place within his premises. Sam took another line.

'What about my business?'

Jack Medlock was already getting bored with hearing it. A young constable had been patiently gathering information regarding Nat Bardsley and his tenancy – 'never a peep 'til this. Still, where does that leave my business, eh?' – but Jack now felt the copper had suffered enough.

'Go away, Mr Middleton. I've apologized for the inconvenience of the investigation. Just be thankful that what's gone on here is *not* your business. Unless you'd like me to consider otherwise and we can start a new line of questioning?'

Middleton took the hint, affected a bruised integrity, and sloped off back into the street where there were plenty of onlookers now gathered ready to hear an account of such an affront to the honest butcher's dignity or, preferably, to pick up a few even more juicy morsels from the doings within.

Jack Medlock considered. So Bernard Cartwright had come here and slain his wife's lover then gone home and struck her a blow that had killed her. Or was it the other way round? No, because she had been here to witness her husband's murderous attack, surely. Otherwise, why the blood all over Alice's clothes? But if that were the case, then why had Bernard taken his wife home to kill her there? And what about the medallion?

So far it didn't make much sense. Bernard himself had said nothing on the walk back along the canalside apart from at one point when he'd turned to Jack and said simply, 'I'm sorry'. It was as if the apology were for some minor inconvenience he'd caused to put a crease in the policeman's otherwise wrinkle-free day.

Sorry? For killing his wife and, possibly, her lover – though until a body was found that was merely speculation – or sorry for binding Jack Medlock within an oath, the reasoning behind which Bernard Cartwright had yet to explain?

Jack Medlock recorded every aspect of the blood-caked room as if it were a new entry in the photograph album in his mind before setting out for the station once more. It was time to put an end to speculation and have a proper talk with Bernard Cartwright.

Jack almost concluded the thought with 'man to man' but smiled coldly as he modified the condition. Square Dealer to Square Dealer.

'I can offer you tea and not much else, I'm afraid.' Jack sat on the edge of the bed that Bernard Cartwright vacated as the policeman had let himself into the cell.

Bernard now stood, his weight against the cell wall, arms

Beryl Baines minds the Cartwright children in happier times.

folded, eyes hard and red-rimmed. He seemed to be waiting, considering some possible, devious catch, before taking the grubby, scalding mug that Jack held up to him.

'Very kind.'

Jack took a deep breath and sank back against the wall.
'Right. I'm listening.'

And so Bernard Cartwright began to speak.

An hour later and Jack Medlock had hardly offered a word as
the mill owner's story poured forth. There was a long silence
in the room before Jack leaned forward on the meagre,
threadbare mattress, head down, elbows resting on his
knees. Jack looked as tired as the man standing over him. He
drew one deep breath and stood, then took a step towards
Bernard Cartwright who had, from the beginning of his sorry
tale, not once moved from his leaning position against the
wall. Jack's whispered words sounded closer to a hiss. His
patience had worn just a little too thin.

'You asked me if I'd deal square, Cartwright. You used
those words and we both know what they mean. I'll be back
when you stop messing me about.'

With that he clanged his way angrily out of the cell, no
longer interested in waiting to see Bernard Cartwright drop
heavily onto the bed, his hands now covering his face, or to
hear the deep sobs that rocked the big man's chest.

Bernard Cartwright's brain pounded inside his skull with a
sickening insistence that the most relentless machinery in his
factory could never have matched. He'd told his tale and
hoped it would be enough yet it had been the thin concoction
of a naïve man who had prided himself throughout his life on
simple, straightforward honesty.

Bernard would have insisted right then that he'd thought
his story through clearly; how he'd followed his suspicions all
the way to that bloody staircase where he'd struck out in a
wild and jealous frenzy then disposed of the body, how then
he'd returned home to confront his wife with the deed and in
the blur of her subsequent hysteria he'd struck her what
turned out to be – though he'd never intended such an

outcome – a deadly blow to the head. This wasn't how he'd foreseen the policeman's response. Bernard had admitted it, hadn't he? What more did the man want?

Yet Bernard knew, even during the telling of his story, as the fog of horror slowly cleared inside his mind that this Jack Medlock was no fool and would expect far more. Bernard had invoked the code of the their mutual Brotherhood but even so, he realized now, he couldn't expect the man to sit there and swallow the half-thought out fantasy that Bernard had tried, with rapidly diminishing enthusiasm, to feed him.

All Bernard knew was that Alice was dead and he'd killed her and for that, by all the rules he'd ever believed in, he deserved to die. They would hang him, he was sure. Who would believe he'd not meant to hurt her, this woman who must have laughed behind her husband's back and from within the hot sheets of her lover's bed, and he the foreman at Bernard Cartwright's own mill.

Bernard saw years of imprisonment, an unthinkable notion, stretching out in a vast emptiness before him.

His children would know only shame whatever the outcome, yet, in his heart, Bernard saw that the one, last useful thing he could do, the only thing he could leave behind, was to spare Alice that shame. Medlock must believe that the whole bloody business sprang from Bernard's own insane and unfounded jealousy; that his wife was innocent, of everything.

Bernard did not even notice the cell door open. How long had it been? An hour? Half a day?

And now Jack Medlock was back. The little policeman closed the cell door then turned and tossed something towards Bernard that the bigger man caught automatically as it flew across the front of his face.

'Yours?'

Bernard looked at the thing in his hand. It was a medallion on a broken chain. Some symbol he didn't recognize.

'I've never seen it before.'

Jack took the thing and slipped it back into his pocket. 'Just wondered. Thought you might've dropped it, you know . . .'

Bernard reddened. 'I'm sorry about all that business by the canal. I panicked. I'd no idea what I was going to do with myself.'

'Not the viaduct, then?' Jack's tone was almost gentle. Bernard thought about the prospect. It had never entered his mind, not consciously anyway. Or had it?

'No.'

The two men looked at each other for what seemed to Bernard Cartwright a painfully long time. Jack Medlock, too, felt the silence but he was determined he would not be the one to break it.

'Had I best start again?'

Jack tried not to show the inner sigh of relief he felt at these words. For some unknown reason he felt terribly sorry for this big, confused man standing before him.

'I think you better had.'

Bernard Cartwright sank onto the little stool that now made up the only other furniture in the room. Medlock must have brought it in with him, Bernard thought. Had he always planned to stay longer this time? It didn't matter. Nothing mattered any more. Except the children. Bernard forced himself not to cry any more. What about the children?

Bernard Cartwright began his story once again.

This time there was no hint of Jack Medlock storming out of the cell in frustration. As Bernard's slow and careful account drew to its conclusion in the fracas on the canal bank earlier that day, the only thing the inspector could do was shake his head slowly from side to side. Bernard waited.

'If you lied to me before – after you'd good as sworn when we were out there on the canal you'd tell it straight – why should I be expected to believe what you've just told me now?'

It was a fair question, Bernard knew, and he wished he had a convincing response.

'Because that's all I've got left.'

Jack pondered this a moment then stood as if to clear his head and get a better view of the facts.

Fred Platt approached the cell.

'Mr Medlock, sir? There's all kinds of folk making a big stink about seeing this . . . er, Mr Cartwright, sir. Some lawyer from somewhere, ranting and raving.'

'Tell him to wait.' Bernard Cartwright's natural authority in such circumstances rose in spite of himself.

'Tell them all to wait.' Jack confirmed the order. 'They'll have plenty to go at soon enough.'

And so Jack Medlock listened as Bernard Cartwright laid out the terms of his final request to a brother Square Dealer.

The policeman had never been faced with a more awful bargain.

The Inspector and the Doctor

'No sign of whatever it was he clobbered her with?'

'Not so far.'

'Or the body of the other bloke . . . what's his name . . . Bardsley?'

Jack Medlock felt the prickle of discomfort under his collar. His superiors on the force he could probably deal with. They'd swallow whatever he chucked at them if it meant a quick conviction and a slate wiped clean. Jim Hadfield was different. He was a clever and cynical man who, despite his affection for Jack, only believed in evidence confirmed for him by his own eyes. Even then he'd check.

'And the great detective's theory?'

From anyone but Jim, Jack would have taken this tone as

New shops now occupy the site of Nat Bardsley's murder.

calculated to insult but he knew that his friend had the greatest respect for Jack's powers as a solver of criminal mysteries. The respect was mutual.

'Cartwright goes to see Bardsley, expecting to find his wife. They have a row, as you'd expect.'

Jim's slight, almost Gallic, shrug of the shoulders acknowledged the obvious. Jack went on, 'Cartwright kills Bardsley and is in the process of getting rid of the body when the wife appears and goes crazy.'

'Again, as you might expect.' Jack shot the doctor a look at this latest interruption. Jim smiled in apology and let the policeman go on with the story.

'She goes crazy, attacks Cartwright, tries to scratch his eyes out, whatever, he swings out to fend her off and kills her, accidentally or otherwise. He gets rid of the man's body and in whatever mixed-up state he's in, takes the wife's body home. I've seen stranger.'

Jim sensed from the pause that this was all that was on offer. 'So he *just happens* to bash her hard enough with whatever he *just happens* to be holding in his hand at the time to cause a depressed skull fracture. Hmm. And then he gets rid of one body while making a point of leaving the other out in the open where anybody can find it. Why not either get rid of both or leave both where they are?'

'It's complicated, I admit.' Jack Medlock was getting a sense of what Bernard Cartwright must have felt trying to sell the same story.

The body of Alice Cartwright lay in apparent, untroubled sleep between them. Only the broken, purplish indentation below her hairline, so incongruous against the pale smoothness of her face, gave any indication that her true state was something rather different.

'I take it he's right-handed, this Cartwright?'

Jack Medlock winced. He'd been waiting for this. 'No.'

Jim looked up from his studious examination of the young woman's otherwise unmarked face, his round face forming a quizzical smile. 'Then it really is complicated, isn't it?'

Jack Medlock nodded his head like a schoolboy caught cheating in a test. Jim Hadfield began to peel off his gloves. 'Drink?'

Jack followed the doctor out of the examining room and into a small, untidy office. The outcome of the case and the progress, or otherwise, of Jack Medlock's career now hung by the thread of this man's confidence. Would it hold? There was no other choice.

The whisky was of exceptional quality, as always, but Jack didn't bother to sip it as it deserved. The first one disappeared in one quick tip of the head. The doctor was awaiting the real story just as Jack had done earlier. This time Jack would have to include the chapter dealing with his own dilemma.

The doctor listened intently, nodding occasionally but never venturing either comment or question. The appearance of Tommy Sykes – it seemed so long ago now – and the pursuit and apprehension of Bernard Cartwright were all dealt with quickly enough.

Jack then paused and poured himself another drink, duty could wait. 'When I got to the house, she was there on the table just like my blokes had said. It was as if he'd expected her to wake up. I had a look round. You saw the blood on her dress. Obviously it wasn't hers from the state of the body, there was just that, really . . . the wound on her head. Apart from that . . . just a few bits on the floor. Stuff that'd got knocked about. Nothing all that special. Apart from this.'

Jack produced the medallion from his pocket like a reluctant magician. 'It was Bardsley's. Used to wear it round his neck, apparently. Some kind of gypsy good-luck charm.'

Jim took it and again raised an eyebrow. Jack went on.

'I know. Didn't do him much good, did it. Anyway, his mate identified it as being his. Never took it off, he said. So . . . I'm thinking, what's this doing on Cartwright's kitchen floor? I showed it to him. Never seen it before in his life. And I believe him. He caught it with his left hand, by the way. Handwriting's left handed as well, by the looks of it.'

'So what's the real tale?'

Jack went on to tell the story as he believed it had happened, as he'd now been told, from Bernard finding his wife and the slain body of her lover to the two encounters in the cell earlier that day. How Bernard had disposed of Nat Bardsley's body with a certain macabre appropriateness in the temporary crematorium of Cartwright's boiler-room because of the scratch-marks on the man's face that bore the evidence of Alice's guilt. And how Alice had cracked her skull on the sharp corner of the big, oak table during her wild breaking-out from the seemingly catatonic state induced by her shock at her earlier actions.

Jim Hadfield took all this in. 'So why try and palm me off

with the first version? I mean, how long have we known one another, Jack?'

Jack looked suitably chastened. 'You see . . . that's the complicated part.'

How was he going to put this? It was time for another visit to the bottle.

'So you're telling me . . .' Jim Hadfield was struggling to organize what he'd heard into something he could get to grips with, '. . . you're going to let Cartwright hang himself on the strength of him trying to save his wife's reputation when you know it's all just a tale.'

'Summat like that.' Jack wished the truth, when laid out so openly by his friend, didn't sound so weak and insubstantial. Bernard Cartwright would let it be known that his mistrust of his wife had been unfounded, that there was not the slightest scrap of evidence that she and Nat were lovers, as he'd believed in his mad jealousy. That the whole thing was the figment of his own tortured and twisted imagination. She had never been near Nat Bardsley's house. He would insist to the world that Alice had been faithful to the last and that he, Bernard, had committed an act of insanity for which he must now atone.

'And all because the pair of you swore some silly oath so as you could get a pay rise, or an alderman's chain once you're too old to care one way or the other.'

'It's not like that.'

But Jim Hadfield was angry now. 'That's exactly what it's like. If anybody finds out what you're doing, they'll lock you up, man, never mind him.'

Jack had no reply. Everything Jim was saying was true, he couldn't deny it. Jack was letting a man condemn himself to certain execution over a matter of honour; Bernard's own in the single purpose of saving his wife's name, Jack's in allowing the man to cling to the sole vestige of dignity left to him and going against his own sworn duty as a policeman to keep his oath to the Square Dealers. Jack never dreamed those convivial evenings in the company of bluff, self-important businessmen in the smoky lodge-rooms would ever lead to this. Still, the oath he'd sworn to come to the aid of his fellows surely meant this, or it meant nothing.

Jim didn't understand any of it and said so firmly enough. A heavy silence lingered between the two men until Jack could wait no longer.

'What will you do?'

Jim drained his glass and banged it down onto the worn surface of his desk. He made no attempt to hide his distaste for what he'd heard. 'What will I do? What d'you think, Jack? Let the bloody pair of you hang yourselves, I suppose. If that's what you want.'

He went to the door and paused, half-way across the threshold. 'Best get this farce wrapped up, then, hadn't we.'

Elsewhere

'Mrs Collier?'

Sergeant Fred Platt and Constable Whittaker stood stamping and shivering outside the door of a little terraced house on Nelson Street. The woman who answered the door did not come up to the expectations stirred by the fellow copper who'd first taken Annie Collier's name in the factory two days earlier.

'I'm her mam, Mrs Weaver. What you after?'

'Could we speak to her, please, madam?' Fred Platt was a stickler for decorum. 'We have come to the right address, I take it?'

'Aye, you have but she's not in.'

'Have you any idea when she might be back?'

'Dunno. She were havin' a bit o' time off work. She's gone out.'

Fred sensed the conversation beginning to trace a circular path that might keep them out here freezing for the rest of the morning.

'Would you mind telling her we've been and that somebody from the station might be wanting to speak to her. We'll call again.'

And with that the two policemen gratefully headed back in the direction of the nearest police box where they were sure to find the means of producing a much needed brew.

'I don't see the point, now, anyway. Bloke's admitted it. "Cut-Throat Cartwright" they're callin' him now. Job's done and dusted.' Constable Whittaker was still able to ward off some of the cold with what remained of the glow of heroism that he'd attempted – without too great an insistence – to brush off in the presence of his admiring colleagues.

'What Mr Medlock wants, he gets, as far as I'm concerned. And if you want to get beyond constable, lad, you'll learn that pretty damn quick.'

But Mr Medlock did not seem, on this occasion, to want to follow his usual relentless pursuit of every strand left to be tied in any case that ever crossed his chaotic desk. In fact, Mr Medlock appeared more than a little tetchy of late. The job did indeed appear to be done and dusted. Cartwright was guilty. Simple as that. The story of the events of Christmas Night and Boxing Day had been duly broadcast and established as holy writ around the station and now the matter had entered the province of newspaper and public speculation, the one, sadly, no more restrained or rational than the other.

The trial date was set. A formality, it was said, and in the event, so it proved. Jack Medlock gave his account and James Campbell Hadfield declared, with all the authority he'd earned from an impeccable reputation that encompassed a number of such cases, that Alice Rafferty had indeed died from a heavy impact fracturing her skull. This much was true. The doctor had seen, to his great relief, no occasion to perjure himself. His appearance on the stand was brief and his sin, had it been noted, was merely one of omission.

Bernard Cartwright was sentenced to hang, by the neck,

until dead – and may God rest his soul. The expression on Bernard's face, throughout the judge's declaration, never changed from a blank and bovine acceptance. It was the will of the court that he be taken from this place . . .

Somewhere around that point, Jack Medlock remembered, he began to feel physically sick and had to slip, he hoped unnoticed, from the back of the courtroom. He had stood by and watched men in makeshift rings punch and beat each other to a red and gory pulp but his stomach had never turned as it did on that day.

In early January, her appointment with the Weatherfield Police long forgotten, Annie Collier arrived at Liverpool docks and boarded a steamship bound for Philadelphia with a cargo of machine parts and threadbare families who would be sustained throughout the long voyage on the hope of a better life, if little else. It was unusual for a young woman to be travelling alone. Still, as the gathered wives in steerage were quick to observe, that one wouldn't be on her own for long.

They did not know – how could they? – that Annie Collier had changed. She had no time any more for the crewmen and wide boys who came sniffing at her so openly. Her heart just wasn't in it.

Finally

It was many months before Jack Medlock's men felt that their boss had returned to something resembling his old self. Jim Hadfield felt it too but unlike everyone else, he knew what lay behind the shortness of temper, the impatience and the apparent lack of focus.

In the days leading up to Bernard Cartwright's execution, Jack had cut more corners and bent more rules on behalf of the condemned man than he would ever do again for all those combined who subsequently crossed his path.

Eyebrows were raised in the corridors of power. Questions were muttered along the same corridors and no doubt behind the doors they led off to. But Jack Medlock's reputation proved sufficient armour against disapproval, implied or stated. He was an honourable man, after all. Everyone knew that much. You'd trust old Jack with your life.

In spite of himself, Jack Medlock could not have prevented a rueful smile at the thought.

Family, business associates, lawyers and those entrusted with the maintenance of the Cartwright empire came and went.

Bernard Cartwright went about leaving the world in as ordered a state as he would have liked to see it were he to remain. Every eventuality was provided for. He seemed quietly resigned to what lay in store, the only hint of sadness crossing his otherwise passive countenance was at the mention of his three children.

They had, as requested, been entrusted to the care of Bernard's sister, Clara, who was childless. Her husband, serious, hard-working Harry Fairclough, was a buyer for the company, working out of a small office in Liverpool. Bernard had always said he was a good man. The children would prosper if, as was his only remaining hope, they could emerge from the shadow their father had cast over them.

At least Amelia was too young to know. One day Clara would tell her. The boys were confused. He would try to tell them himself. Exactly what, he didn't yet know. Something.

Jack Medlock arranged – and nobody at the station could believe how he'd managed it – for Bernard Cartwright to be brought back from Preston, where he was being held before the execution, to Weatherfield to meet his two sons. They were to walk unattended in the park with Jack Medlock and two edgy constables in close-as-need-be attendance.

Jack sat in the bandstand, freezing but not caring. He'd instructed the men accompanying him to refrain from comment unless it was absolutely essential, pulled his collar up and sunk into the depths of his coat to wait – he also informed the constables to their chagrin – as long as it took.

Jack would always look back on that day as a painting. Snow still covering the normally green expanse of the park. Blue-grey sky. Bare trees. And three black silhouette figures, one almost too big next to the others, moving, then standing. Apart, then so close together as to be one lumpy, blurring smudge against the white background. For one brief instant he thought he'd seen a flickering fourth image then he'd dismissed it as the dark flapping of a coat and the glare of the sunlight off the snow.

Jack never heard a word Bernard Cartwright said to the two boys in all the time the three were together. He never asked and the condemned man never offered anything other than a simple thanks. As heart-felt and as true as anything Jack Medlock had ever been given in his life. Thanks.

And so Bernard Cartwright was taken back to his Preston cell and on the morning of April 12th he was hanged.

Inspector Medlock, the arresting officer in charge of the case, was not present at the execution.

A week after the death of Bernard Cartwright, as the newspapers' interest waned and the people's minds turned with an equal readiness from murder to the prospect of finer weather, Jack Medlock still hadn't got round to clearing his desk of the ephemera of the Cartwright Case. The business was now entrenched in local legend as the crazy act of a madman – long-since christened Cut-Throat Cartwright – whose insane jealousy brought about the deaths of two tragic innocents whose only crime, as all the evidence indicated, was the exchange of the occasional social pleasantry. A little indiscreet, perhaps, but nothing more. Such a waste.

Men shook their heads and women nodded to each other in the ancient knowledge that it's always the quiet ones. Beyond that and the invention of a few wildly embellished scare stories for the benefit of erring children, life returned to normal with a reassuring readiness. Jack Medlock found it all deeply depressing.

Though he seemed to thrive in it and, others would contend, have a knack of creating it around himself, Jack hated untidiness. In his view, however, the ordered state – or otherwise – of his office was of secondary importance to the ordered state of his mind. He had consigned an indecent number of official-looking papers to the waste basket that morning before hesitating over a torn scrap that bore only a name and address. Why Jack felt it to be significant just then he could not have said, yet he was puzzled by something or other and he wouldn't rest until he'd found out what it was.

The inspector firmly believed that if an itch persisted enough to need scratching there was something causing it that needed to be cleared up.

He approached Fred Platt, who was currently hunched in rapt concentration over what Jack saw to be the racing page. That was before his sergeant whisked it out of sight under the counter.

'What did we end up doing about this, Fred?'

Jack slipped the paper onto the counter for Fred's consideration. The sergeant sifted through dimly-lit memory banks, desperate not to appear wanting, before gratefully lighting upon the connection.

'Collier . . . right . . . yes, sir. We called round, wasn't in at the time, sir. We were due to call back but by that time old Cut- er, Mr Cartwright had come clean over the whole business, sir. I didn't really want to mither you with it after that and then we dragged that young . . . kid out of the canal at the end of January and it all got a bit . . . shoved to one side, sir, if you see what I mean. Er, sorry, Mr Medlock.'

Jack nodded and studied the paper again as if he might have missed something. 'Never mind, Fred. Not your fault.'

Fred Platt was mightily relieved as he watched his boss

wander back inside the little office. As the door clicked shut, Fred even felt safe enough to return to his inner moral debate over whether Danny Boy in the 2:15 at Manchester was worth a small slice of his meagre sergeant's wages.

On a warmer day, much later, some twenty odd years, in fact, a tall young woman with striking green eyes and a mass of unruly red hair entered the cemetery grounds of the small Catholic church of St Aidan and Oswald in Weatherfield. She was carrying a bunch of flowers – lilacs – and a book of poems by William Shakespeare.

When she reached the grave of her mother, the woman noticed a stony-faced little man, mid-fifties she would guess later, wearing a trilby hat and belted mackintosh. He was lingering close to the graveside.

The man had not noticed the young woman's approach and appeared startled as her shoes crunched on the gravel no more than a few feet away. He turned to leave but her voice pulled him up.

'Have I seen you before?' There was no hint of aggression in her directness. Jack Medlock turned to face her and in an instant felt he could grow to like this young woman very quickly. The way she fixed you with eyes that, no matter how formal the circumstance, would always hold the promise of a smile not too far below the surface. First Alice, now Amelia.

He hesitated. 'I knew your father.'

The promised smile sank a little further into the distance. 'D'you mind if I ask what you're doing here?'

Jack had often wondered the same thing himself. 'I promised him I'd make sure Alice's grave was kept tidy.' It sounded so inadequate as a reason for being here in violation of someone else's private world.

'I do that,' she said simply.

'I know you do.' He shrugged. 'You've saved me a job all this time.'

Now the smile. Just. She began to replace the week-old

flowers in the fixed vase under the white marble headstone.
A diversion.

'Were you friends? With my dad, I mean?'

'No. Not friends. I arrested him.'

Amelia looked up, holding the dying flowers as she waited
for him to go on.

'He wasn't what people thought he was, you know, your
dad.'

Jack realized that he was drifting into a tangled mass of
explanations for which he'd not come prepared and which
might leave this woman having to reassess the way she saw
her whole life. He couldn't let that happen. Why hadn't he just
run away the second he saw her? As the panic welled up
inside Jack's chest, and it occurred to him he'd faced armed
villains with far less concern, Amelia Cartwright rescued
him.

'Would it bring either of them back?' The question took him
by surprise. Jack's puzzled expression was her cue to go on.
'If you tell me stories about my parents, what they were like,
even what you think was supposed to have happened, it
wouldn't make any difference, would it? It wouldn't change
anything. They'd still both be long gone.'

She looked at him as if needing to explain to a clumsy but
well-meaning child. It was how he was beginning to feel. 'I'd
go to both their graves if I could, Mr . . . no don't tell me. I'd
rather not know, if you don't mind. I've lived with it this long.
I've heard all kinds of stories. And you know what, I think they
loved one another. Why look surprised? I don't know what
happened and I don't think anybody does, really, but . . . I
know this sounds strange and you'll probably think I'm mad . . .
my mam and dad, whatever they had between them . . . well
. . . that's me now, isn't it. Any good that's in me comes from
them. And you know something else, I don't hate anybody,
me. It's not in me and I've no time for it. Don't ask me why but
I know . . . in here . . .' At this Amelia made a sudden
passionate gesture that Jack Medlock took to include not just

her heart or her head but her whole being. '. . . they loved one another. That's all I need to know. Nothing anybody will ever say about it is going to make any difference now. To me or them.'

She bent to place the new flowers in the vase and Jack watched as she spent a few seconds spreading the blooms to her satisfaction. When the task was completed she stood once more, taller than Jack, he noticed for the first time, and smiled her real and wonderful smile at last.

'I didn't mean to be rude.'

'You weren't.'

'My dad must've trusted you.'

If only he could tell her. Still, it was better this way; the way she wanted it, the way she'd dealt with it.

'Aye. I think we could have been friends, you know, if . . .'

She looked at him, smiling, and it made him feel that if he didn't leave now her eyes and his own guilt might turn him to stone and leave him to watch over Alice's grave for ever. Jack felt it might not be too unjust a fate, all things considered.

'Thank you.' That was all she said. Jack knew it was sincere and that in the single phrase she was willing to write off the debt of over twenty years. It was also an invitation to leave her alone and he took it with a gracious nod of the head, leaving Amelia standing quite still above her mother's grave. Jack Medlock would always picture her thus, almost a statue herself now but for the breeze gently lifting her long red hair.

He never saw her again. As Jack walked away through the gravestones he thought only of another woman – perhaps even more beautiful than this Amelia – though he'd no recollection of her alive. He saw her laid out in such seeming peace on a hard oak table and he saw the brass-bound coffin that held her, lowered into the frozen ground days after. He saw, too, his own sorry presence at the graveside, reaching into the pocket of his overcoat to take out the medallion on its broken chain and in his mind's eye he caught the glint of it now, as he had watched it then, falling from his hand onto the wooden box, soon to disappear forever under the earth.

PART 3

WEATHERFIELD, SUMMER 2000

And that, it seemed, was that. As I sipped a half in the Rovers Return, surrounded by an untidy array of notes, cuttings and documents I reflected on how, in the late spring of 1898, Weatherfield had gradually returned to normal. Recent events in our own neighbourhood, those that had set this whole investigation under way, in fact, had shown how that could happen. Life went on then in much the same way as it does today.

With the demise of Bernard Cartwright, the local people could now sleep safe in their beds, secure in the belief that justice had been done and the cut-throat ogre had been despatched to a well-deserved fate. Older residents of the town still recall to this day the dreaded name being used to chasten wayward children for many a year after. Cut-Throat Cartwright'll have you if you don't behave.

In all parts of the north, the bogeyman has a name usually associated with local crime: Bill O'Jacks, Tom Pepper, Billy Binks. And so, added to the list – sadly but naturally enough, folk being what they are – was the name of Bernard Cartwright.

As all the evidence showed, the accepted wisdom at the time was that Bernard Cartwright had confronted his wife about her infidelity with Nat Bardsley. The pair then had a heated argument that resulted in Bernard striking his wife and, whether it had been the intention or not, killing her. He'd then gone out into the night, remorse driving him to insanity, determined to wreak vengeance on his wife's lover. He had broken into the butcher's shop and cold-bloodedly slashed Nat Bardsley's throat with a knife from the shop that was never found. The murderer disposed of the body and even as the noose tightened on his own neck, persisted in his arrogant refusal to reveal its whereabouts. In the act of disposing of his wife's body, Bernard then fled the scene, and the police, who finally apprehended him by the canal. He was tried and executed for his crime and order, it was felt, had been restored.

Most of the above we have seen to be inaccurate, if not totally false. Much of the blame for that can only be laid at the doors of Bernard himself and his co-conspirator, Jack Medlock. The version that was shared by Jack and the coroner, James Campbell Hadfield was altogether different.

Alice Cartwright, said by some to have had, in her youth, a violent temper when crossed, went to meet Nat Bardsley in a jealous rage over his dalliance with another woman. The two had fought and their argument had taken them into the butcher's shop below Nat's rooms. He may have hit her, she scratched his face, they struggled. She picked up a sharpened cleaver from the block on the counter and swung out wildly. The blow caught Nat across the throat and killed him almost instantly. Bernard Cartwright had found his wife, near-paralysed by the shock of what she'd done. He took her home and she had been galvanized by a fit of remorse, becoming wild and incoherent. Bernard had tried to quiet her and in the struggle, she'd fallen and hit her head, dying instantly. He had disposed of Nat Bardsley's body because it bore the damning evidence of the struggle with Alice.

Bernard had then prevailed on Jack, drawing on their shared affiliation to the Square Dealers, to allow him to take the blame for both deaths in order to protect his wife's name from association with the murder of Nat Bardsley and lay the motive at Bernard's own door as one of mad jealousy founded on no factual evidence; that he had been wrong about his wife and his works' foreman from the first. It was the only way Bernard could see of saving his wife's name, not only for her own but for their children's sake. He blamed himself for her death, insisting he had as good as killed her,

132

that he deserved to die as a result and that he was resigned to the consequences.

Jack confided in Hadfield that a kind of madness had possessed Bernard Cartwright in those last days of his life but that the madness carried a methodical, twisted kind of logic that the unfortunate man was determined to cling on to, even in the face of his own execution. Above all else, and unto the very last, Bernard Cartwright felt that he had, for better or worse, done the right thing. He had 'dealt square'.

So, two versions of the same tale. I began to construct the second one, the 'story' previously related, based on all the evidence I'd found over months of digging. I was pleased with myself. I was sure I'd uncovered the innocence of an unfortunate, tragic man, caught in a cruel dilemma and with no more will to live after, he believed, he had brought on his wife's death. I was satisfied that, through what had been newly uncovered, a kind of justice had been done on Bernard's behalf.

Yet in all I'd unravelled of the character of Jack Medlock, all the idiosyncrasies and layers that made up the picture of this complex man, I still felt that something was missing. One wildly flapping loose end kept appearing right before my eyes and I couldn't quite catch hold of it. It was something about Jack Medlock being a better copper than this, or at least a better man.

I felt he could not have been satisfied with the outcome of the story as he'd told it. Neither could I.

There was something wrong. Jack Medlock knew it, though the question is, when did he become certain? If events after the double death hadn't moved so fast and the normally scrupulously thorough policeman had not been caught up in it, I'm sure he would have acted differently.

Whatever the reasons, Jack Medlock's oversight – and we can never truly know when he acknowledged it – provided a fascinating postscript to my investigation and, I believe, tied that maddening loose end. No hard evidence remained, only circumstance and hearsay, the kind of rumour I'd made it my business to either confirm or avoid. And yet I became convinced during the course of my 'reconstruction' that there was a third version of the story still to be told.

I decided to follow and record certain events from the later lives of our surviving protagonists.

But first, the backdrop against which the whole murky business had been played out. What happened to Cartwright's?

The mill was taken over, under instruction of its late owner, by a group of interested parties including Harry Fairclough, who was also acting as guardian of the boys, William and Robert. Harry rose to the position of overall manager of the site and the business soon settled back down to its accustomed routine. Even the seismic tremors of the murder case could not shake the giant from its purpose. Buyers, debtors and creditors alike were soon able to shelve their finer feelings once they'd all admitted to themselves, privately or otherwise, that the only thing that really mattered was money.

Gradually, inevitably, Cartwright's assets began to erode throughout the next thirty years as cheaper manufacturing costs took the industry elsewhere and the cotton mills of the north-west proved themselves fatally slow in spotting the sea change gathering on the horizon.

Cartwright Cotton closed in 1930 taking many of the area's jobs with it. After a succession of failed businesses took over the premises, a local firm re-opened part of the ground floor in 1961 and made a go of turning out switch-gear for heavy machinery but they were soon overtaken themselves by the computer age in an ostrich-manoeuvre that was sadly reminiscent of their longer-lived predecessor. The mill was eventually pulled down in 1972.

Roy Cropper showed me a poignant but splendid collection of photographs charting the slow destruction of the old beast. There is even television footage in an archive in Manchester that records the toppling of the great chimney, though it's years now since I saw it. The demolition man from Bolton who used to present the programme takes great delight in the chimney's slow, crumpling flop to the ground. It seems odd now, looking back, that we watched the destruction of our industrial heritage for entertainment. I suppose today we preserve it, sanitized and safe, for the same purpose.

The site, as all sites seem to do, then spent a number of years as a car-park before ironically contributing to the demise of another common sight in every old town throughout Britain: the corner shop. It was sold to a super-market chain and the current store has become a prominent feature of the local landscape. Its shopping trolleys also became a prominent feature in the local canal for a long time but fortunately, such matters are now under control.

Both William and Robert were soon to meet a fate equally tragic as that of their father.

In 1898, soon after the death of their parents, Clara took the boys to live in Southport, away from the whispers and turning heads of Weatherfield. The boys were bright and did well at school but despite good offers from Cambridge they were determined to become established within their father's busi-ness as soon as possible. This led to heated arguments with Harry, and with Clara who was adamant they should continue their studies.

In the event, the outbreak of war settled the matter. By November 1916, Robert Cartwright was a First Lieutenant in the Weatherfield Pals Regiment – more of them later – that in a famously heroic action had resisted a week of gas attacks and heavy shelling at Beaucourt on the Somme, preventing what was seen as an unstoppable German advance. On the morning of 22 November, Robert was part of an attempt to gain an enemy trench as the first push in a counter-offensive. He was last seen, as was reported in the *Manchester Guardian* a week later, wounded and shouting encourage-ment to his men whilst untangling himself from barbed-wire 'with no more concern than if he were disengaging a bramble'.

The Weatherfield Pals, like those similar nearby regiments from places such as Accrington, Manchester and Salford, were the bright idea of those in Whitehall who felt that it would be easier to get young men to go and fight the Germans if their mates were alongside them throughout. They were proved right. Machine-gun spray and bomb-blast, however, had little regard for these social niceties. Men weren't just slaughtered by the platoon or regiment, they were annihilated by the street, the Labour Club, the football team.

Of the lads of Park Villa, managed incidentally, just before and then long after the war years by one Tommy Sykes, nine of the eleven who played in the Manchester and District Amateur Cup Final of 1912 – and won, 3-1 – were killed on the Somme with the Pals. Of the other two, one lost an arm and the other, Bob Jackson the goal-keeper, never played again after a mustard gas cloud had ravaged his lungs.

William Cartwright survived the engagement that killed his brother only to return to the Somme two years later. Stationed at Pozieres Ridge near Bapaume on 27 March 1918, he was opening a packet of orders that would have told him of his promotion to captain, when a sniper's bullet passed through his neck, killing him before he hit the ground.

Happily, Amelia Cartwright has a longer story. She was a head-turning beauty of seventeen by the time the First World War broke out and no doubt many of the young men who eyed her then went away and never came back to follow up their overtures.

Amelia became a school-teacher, returning to Weatherfield in her early twenties, about the time Jack Medlock met her, to take up a post in a local junior school.

Perhaps it isn't surprising that she waited so long to let a man into her life. She was thirty-nine when she met and married William Elliott in 1936. He was five years her junior and a butcher by trade. The first of their two children, Fred, was born a year later.

By that time, Amelia was a headmistress and Bill had a thriving butcher's shop on Mafeking Street and another in the old Weatherfield Market Hall. Maud Grimes, once a workmate at the *Gazette*, remembers her old headmistress, Mrs Elliott, as a tall and striking-looking woman whose red hair was streaked with silver. She can also remember the woman's fondness for reading the verses of Shakespeare during assembly. To this day, Maud can still quote the song 'Fear no more the heat o' the sun…' from *Cymbeline*. She says it was Mrs Elliott's favourite and remembers how her voice seemed to convey such sadness when she spoke it.

Bill Elliott joined the Army Catering Corps during the Second World War and was once saved from a stray bullet by half a pig that happened to be slung over his shoulder as he crossed a parade ground in North Africa. A loaded pistol had accidentally been fired off during an exercise. To the last, Bill was convinced it was actually a statement of dissatisfaction from some under-nourished Tommy regarding the sorry nature of army rations.

The couple died in the same year, 1969. Bill was first after a long bout of illness. He passed the shops on to his son, Fred. Amelia soon followed. This woman who had witnessed the unassailable might and later the slow destruction of the cotton industry, passed through two world wars and borne the scars of tragedy throughout her life, fell asleep watching a television news report from America on the Woodstock Pop Festival. She never woke up. The neighbour who was with Amelia at the time reported that she hadn't wanted to disturb her friend, sitting as she was, with her eyes closed, smiling.

It was said of Amelia and Bill, by all who knew them, that from the first day they met, the couple truly loved one another. Amelia herself said it was all that mattered.

In order to conclude our story – and perhaps to uncover the last remaining piece of the puzzle – we must go back to the autumn of 1898 and to a small ceremony, if it could be described as such, on the corner of Cartwright Street. A row of bright new shops stands there now but where the plate glass window of W&H Hardware now looks out was once the old street sign bearing the name of the recently-convicted murderer. It had to change, the council decreed, out of respect for the feelings of those connected to the victims. There is no evidence that the people of Weatherfield could have cared one way or the other but the council nevertheless acted with the speed they traditionally reserve for matters of little importance and settled, after lengthy debate no doubt, on Victoria Street as the new name. It would probably keep the postman focused, if little else.

Jack Medlock's memoirs tell us that he walked past on that day and saw the old plaque being unscrewed to be replaced by the new one. Maybe this was a piece of literary licence on Jack's part but nevertheless, he must have felt that the Cartwright Case would haunt him wherever he went unless he could somehow lay the ghost forever. A passage from his book states,

> 'It was as though Bernard himself were telling me that here was another humiliation that neither he nor his family deserved.'

Again Jack Medlock as good as declares Bernard Cartwright's innocence. I decided to follow Jack as closely as I could from that moment on, long after the Cartwright Case was officially filed away.

The great escapades that marked Jack Medlock's distinguished career came, for the most part, in the years leading up to and during the First World War after he'd moved from Weatherfield in order to pursue bigger fish in the deeper criminal waters of Manchester.

Before that, in 1899, Jack Medlock took a trip. He had met the woman who was to become his wife only a few months earlier at a civic function and his memoirs tell us that the encounter prompted Jack to follow up his determination to give himself a holiday. The woman, Rose Tanner, had recently lost her husband in the war in South Africa and it seems that the planned trip would provide a welcome tonic for both of them.

Jack took three months leave – he must indeed have been held in high regard – and the couple took a berth on a cruise ship bound for New York.

Jack recounts their visits to a great number of famous tourist attractions with a detective's eye for detail. His account of their excursion by boat to the foot of Niagara Falls is a delightful passage, showing as it does the awe and wonder felt by a man whose life was spent in the industrial north-west for the stunning power and beauty of nature.

He also describes a two-day period during which his companion became rather restless as Jack seemed unable to forget police business entirely. Apparently Jack presented himself at a station of the NYPD on West 54th Street in Manhattan where he spent some time sifting through their records. He also made enquiries of the U.S. Customs and Immigration Service and the Records Office in the state capital, Albany. Then on the second day of his busman's holiday he made the short train journey up the Hudson River from Union Station to Kingston, a small town at the foot of the Catskill Mountains where the Ashokan River joins the Hudson. The huge reservoir nearby provides New York City with its daily drinking water. The episode is passed over as 'most interesting' and Jack describes the scenery with great enthusiasm. He seems to have decided, however, that the purpose of the excursion and the enquiries would not be of interest to the general reader.

And yet, the purpose was of enough importance to leave his new companion to her own devices for the best part of two days in the city. Rose visited museums and art galleries, we are told, where she was apparently much better off without her partner.

I had a hunch that I knew what Jack was up to. I also took a trip.

The passenger records of the now-defunct North Atlantic Steamship Corporation are kept in a small room along an all but forgotten corridor of the Mersey Docks and Harbour Board building in Liverpool. The room smells of once-damp paper long since dried out.

It was from here that I traced Annie Collier's route to America – possibly as Jack Medlock himself had done – along the path that would lead, I believe, to a solution as to what really happened that night in Middleton's Butchers on Cartwright Street.

Annie had gone to Philadelphia. She had taken the first passage available and I began to wonder if the specific destination port had been more important to her than the need to put as many miles between herself and Weatherfield as her combined savings could run to.

Annie Collier had family in America, as many Weatherfielders did and still do. The *Weatherfield Gazette* of 11 May 1895 reports on the emigration of a group of coal-miners from the town who were taking their families to a promised better life. Some were bound for the Pennsylvania coalfields and steel mills, so many of them bearing names brought from the north-west, while others planned to make a living in upstate New York. One among the latter group was a young mining engineer by the name of Sam Weaver. He was Annie's older brother.

I followed my hunch once more to the bowels of the Weatherfield Public Library and the dimly-lit room where they keep the computers. During the course of my research I'd found the internet to be of immeasurable value as a tool for discovery and once again it proved to be just so. I located the telephone directory for the Borough of Kingston in upstate New York and scrolled through the listed names. There were seven Weavers. Maybe none of them would have anything to do with a woman who may or may not have turned up from England over a hundred years ago but then again, maybe one of them just might.

I prepared myself for the inevitability of an outrageous telephone bill at the end of the quarter. It duly arrived but it was worth it.

The first four American Weavers were more than polite but all were unable to help. With the fifth I managed metaphorically what Annie's brother must have hoped for in reality. I struck gold.

Mary-Jane Melvin-Weaver, the charming woman at the other end of the line informed me that 'Great-Aunt Annie' had indeed arrived in Kingston from 'the old country' early in the winter of 1898 – she couldn't say exactly when. In 1910, Annie had met and married a local man but they had no children. I learned much more as I watched the minutes tick away and my phone bill go into orbit but I had found out the one thing I needed to know – the reason for Jack Medlock's trip up the Hudson.

Mary-Jane made enthusiastic enquiries as to the possibility of tracing Weavers in Weatherfield and I promised to help. We even exchanged addresses on the off-chance that the Melvin-Weavers would finally make that trip to England and wished one another the best. Inevitably, she wanted to know if Weatherfield was in London. She seemed rather disappointed when I was obliged to inform her that this was sadly not the case.

Though I could never hope to discover what was said in the meeting between the policeman and the woman whose infatuation with Nat Bardsley had seemingly led to her flight from England, I was able to put together what I believe is a plausible scenario based on the few facts available.

Annie Collier had become obsessed with Nat Bardsley. Unfortunately, she was already married – and to a violent drunkard of a man who thought nothing of striking his wife

whenever he saw fit. We know that Annie disappeared from
Weatherfield immediately after Nat's death and we know that
she fled, via Liverpool, to America where her brother and his
family had set up their new home. Prior to that, apart from the
odd photograph and the trial depositions of witnesses such
as Tommy Sykes – he'd told the court, in the recreation of a
picture of Nat's life, that he thought the deceased was
involved on-and-off with Annie Collier and had given various
reasons for this – we know only of the incident recorded in
police documents for Christmas Night 1897. It was then that a
bruised and battered Annie entered Weatherfield Police
Station and reported an assault carried out on her person by
her husband who, she believed, was currently out somewhere, on the town, still drinking and in foul and violent
temper. As far as immediate connections with the Cartwright
case are concerned, the trail goes cold from that point.
George Collier, Annie's husband, is also conspicuous by his
absence from local events from this point on. At least for a
while. If he'd wanted to trace Annie it would have been far
easier for him, at the time, than it was for me a hundred years
later. I had little difficulty so George could not have been all
that keen to pursue his errant wife. He may have felt she was
better off where she was. In any event, for the time being, it
seems that George Collier, too, had disappeared.

Jack Medlock records that, before he knew the particular
and what he believed for a time to be the true circumstances
of their deaths, he asked Bernard what had led to his suspicions regarding Alice and Nat. Had it been something that
had festered over a long period? Bernard said they'd been
seen together. Not 'he had seen them together'. Jack then
learned of the visit to Cartwright's on Christmas Day from the
strange man who had aroused those suspicions. After that,
the whole thing had come to a head within less than twenty-
four hours. So who was the man?

Bernard had described him as stocky and 'rough-looking',
a nasty piece of work.

A single photograph from the period, in a Collier family album – a posed, indoor portrait before an idyllic, painted Alpine background – shows Annie and her then fiancé, George Collier, smiling dutifully for the camera. She has the look of a naughty and not-quite-grown-up cherub from a Baroque ceiling. He, try as he might to cover it, looks like a dumpy little hard-case with a dull-eyed stare and a cruel twist to his leering mouth.

Why had they fought, that Christmas? We must first look at what led to the fight. It seems that George Collier had gone to confront Nat Bardsley over his relationship with Annie, such as it was. We can be sure that on his trip up the Hudson, Jack Medlock confirmed that Annie had told her husband, probably during the course of one of their plate-smashing rows, who it was she'd been pursuing and fretting over in the weeks leading up to Christmas.

However, whatever his intentions that day, George had turned up on Cartwright Street and found richer pickings. He'd seen Nat Bardsley in heated discussion with Alice Cartwright and it was clear that theirs was more than just a passing acquaintance. George must have decided he could wait to give Nat the good hiding he had planned for him. George now had a new weapon that would do far more damage and one that appealed far more to his nasty, vengeful streak.

He went straight home to inform his wife that her precious fancy-man was at it with someone else – and that someone would certainly keep little factory-hand Annie Collier well out of the picture. He gleefully reported to the devastated Annie that she had been pushed to one side in favour of the boss's wife, Alice Cartwright.

George's next mission was to tell the boss himself and so expose the sordid truth of the whole business. He could then spread the story at leisure once work resumed. As far as George was concerned, if he was going to be cuckolded by Annie – not that he really cared, he had other women he could go to – he may as well poison as many other people's lives as he could in the process.

So Jack Medlock had discovered a sub-plot to the Cartwright Mystery that suddenly, years after, was thrusting itself to the fore and that had to be resolved. Much to his dismay, Jack was beginning to formulate an entirely new theory based on the information he'd learned from Annie Collier and he could not rest until all the ends were tied. He could hardly reopen the case. After all, he'd done so much himself to make sure that it went the way it did. And Bernard had confessed to the double murder. The evidence that condemned him was unassailable. The case had been open and shut. Now it was just plain shut and to reopen it would be career suicide for Jack and would drag the Cartwright name through the mud once more. This time the mud would stick to Alice and he'd sworn to Bernard that he would never let that happen.

I was becoming obsessed myself now, with the need to know what really went on that night – just as Jack must have. I studied every piece of factual evidence in my possession, over and over. I read Medlock's book again. Then Hadfield's lurid novelization of the story his friend had told him years later. Then I re-read my own notes.

It was at this point that I became drawn to a series of photographs that Martha Cribbins had given me, weeks before. They were of her father and, fortunately for my investigation, many of them were dated on the back.

One in particular fascinated me yet I could not work out why.

I knew there was something nagging, there in this portrait of Jack and his new wife, Rose, captured in the first year of the century, looking genuinely happy in each other's company – a quality so lacking in the similar depiction of Annie and George Collier. The photograph is dated March 1900.

It was only after leaving the picture to stare up at me from my own desk top for the best part of a day as I worked, that I noticed the scar. Jack Medlock had acquired a pale, jagged line about an inch long that pulled downwards across his left eyebrow, giving the impression that the eye was slightly closed.

A picture of the couple at a street party on New Year's Eve 1899 shows no such mark. This scar and what I was able to trace of the life of George Collier subsequent to Annie's decamping to the United States, pointed me towards a startling and rather chilling conclusion.

I paid another call on Martha. Luckily, the cat remembered me and affected a cool but vigilant tolerance that granted the humans an afternoon of very fruitful discussion.

I asked Martha about the scar. What she told me seemed, at first, rather vague but it turned out to be most interesting nevertheless. She told me that, as a young child, Martha had more than once asked her dad about the scar across his eye.

In the way of so many elderly people, Martha would forget where she'd put the pension-book she took out specially that morning but she could recall with uncanny accuracy the tiniest events from three quarters of a century past.

She said Jack had told her that a man had hit him – a criminal. When Martha pushed for further details, Jack would only tell her that the man had never hit anybody else again, ever. He would expand no further on the matter but Martha said that her dad would play up the sinister tone of the thing because he knew it gave her a shiver of delight, old Jack painting himself as a real-life version of the Pirate King or Wicked Caliph she so loved in pantomime.

Martha remembered asking – in the innocent way any child might – what had happened to the man. Had he gone to prison for hitting her dad? Jack had told her no but that he'd got what he deserved.

George Collier did, it seems, disappear abroad from Weatherfield immediately after his wife had gone to report him to the police for assaulting her. In those less-enlightened times, the Weatherfield Constabulary probably considered a case of domestic battery hardly worth following up. The Colliers' situation on that night was no doubt being enacted all over the town in much the same way. Husbands hitting their wives was a depressingly familiar scenario in a time when to articulate a sense of frustration was to go for the easy option of striking out with a clenched fist. Anything else might have been seen as less than manly.

We hear nothing of George Collier until well after the storm surrounding the Cartwright murders has settled. Then he makes a dramatic reappearance.

The *Weatherfield Gazette* informs us that in the winter of 1899 – he must have crept back to his old haunts not long before – George Collier received a suspended sentence for his involvement in a street fight that left one man crippled for life and two more hospitalized. In those days the main weapon of the street brawler was the pair of iron-rimmed clogs on his feet. They could do devastating harm to any opponent. Razor-blades in the peak of a flat cap were another, nastier option. A quick swipe across the cheek from some thug's cap could lead to twenty stitches and the bloody end to a confrontation within a second. There were rumours, in George Collier's case, of a war between organized gangs vying for dominance in the lucrative barge transport of stolen goods down the canal but nothing of that nature stuck to those involved in the fracas.

It is a fact that George Collier was established as a local ne'er-do-well around Weatherfield in the early months of the twentieth century when he appears – in what were seen at the time as puzzling circumstances – to have met a violent end.

The newspaper reports, spread over a period in January 1900, tell us that a man was dragged from the Bridgewater Canal on the morning of 16 January. He was later identified as George Collier and the cause of death appears to have been drowning. The coroner, not James Campbell Hadfield in this case, recorded, however, that the man was a probably unconscious when he entered the water. Collier's face had been battered to a near pulp by repeated blows. The man's own knuckles showed signs of severe abrasions. Whatever had gone on, the coroner returned a verdict of death by misadventure and there is no evidence of any enthusiastic pursuit by the Weatherfield police of any other parties to the incident. It was felt that the community was rid of a bad apple and it was those still lurking in the barrel that had brought it about. Collier's known criminal associates were all discounted.

Nobody, it seems, was ever brought to trial or even questioned about the death. Collier's family, led by a sister, Dorothy, kicked up a fuss at the time, naturally enough, but they were only too aware of the company George kept and any deep investigation might make certain surviving clan members rather uncomfortable in light of their own dubious money-making activities. The case was soon closed. The officer who had followed the illegal doings of George Collier with most interest in the lead-up to his death that January was Jack Medlock, yet by early February, as his memoirs relate, Jack had moved on to other things.

George Collier's death on 16 January falls between the two photographs of Jack Medlock, the one without, then the one with, the scar. The March picture would have given any wound on Jack's face, picked up in mid-January, at least six weeks to heal beyond bruising, swelling or stitches, to a neat scar such as the one he had mysteriously acquired from the man who, Jack would tell his daughter in such arch tones, had 'hit him'.

A new picture of events was becoming clearer in my mind. I discussed my suspicions, as to what might have happened involving Jack, with Martha. I laid out a revised version of the story, from the death of Nat Bardsley to the death of George Collier, that seemed to explain all the unconnected events in between and tie up the loose ends of the tale. I could not include it in my book without her permission. To my great relief, she believed the account that follows to be the truth and so do I.

The Cartwright Murders: Last Word

Some will see this as a mystery solved. Some might say there are more questions still to be answered. All I will contend is that every one of the facts available pointed me towards a remarkable conclusion – and they are there, for anybody who so wishes, to pick them up after me and interpret them as they will.

On Christmas Day 1897, the vengeful George Collier thought it a fine extra Christmas present to give to his unfaithful wife, Annie, the details of her lover's secret affair with the wife of Bernard Cartwright. Instead of the cold anger he'd harboured for weeks, here was a chance to gloat and watch his wife's anguish as her cherished fantasy crumbled about her. Leaving Annie to come to terms with the fact that she was being kept out of Nat Bardsley's affections by another woman, George went to find Bernard Cartwright and give him the news that his own wife was having an affair, thereby enacting what he saw as a more fitting revenge on Nat Bardsley than the beating he'd once planned for him. Maybe George reckoned to go back and confront Nat another day but events soon took a different turn.

After his visit to Cartwright's mill and his encounter with the stunned owner, George Collier went out to get drunk and celebrate his twisted little victory.

George returned home late that night. He was blind drunk having spent the whole day – in what the local pubs still euphemistically call a 'private party' in order to bypass licensing laws – doling out his Christmas wages across a bar.

Whatever shade his mood took on the way home, it darkened when he found his wife waiting for him in some distress. He might have been perversely satisfied had her concern been that she was deprived of her husband's company throughout the best part of Christmas Day. In George's mind that would have served her right. But Annie had not stayed at home bemoaning her feckless husband's absence. She had gone in search of Nat Bardsley in order to find out if George's gloating tale was true and that Nat had indeed taken up with Alice Cartwright. Indeed she may also have gone in search of Nat on Christmas Eve, swearing she would leave her husband if Nat would take her. It could have been this meeting that delayed Nat's drinking rendezvous with Tommy.

On Christmas Night, she had gone out after dark and found Nat at home again – reading, of all things – and railed at him until he'd admitted that, yes, he was in love with the boss's wife and there was certainly no future for Annie in his life. She flew into a rage at the news and raked Nat's face with her nails – scratching him quite badly, she'd realized afterwards – then stormed out of the butcher's shop in floods of tears.

George Collier had laughed, telling his wife she was well served and that should be an end of it. But Annie insisted that she was in love with Nat and would not give up so easily. Her husband was a vile, drunken pig and she wanted nothing more to do with him, regardless of what Nat Bardsley currently felt. Nat would change, she was convinced. She could make him change.

George's drunken satisfaction at his wife's misfortune was now transformed into a violent rage. He slapped her hard across the side of the head and Annie, not unaccustomed to seeing him in this state and still simmering with her own anger, retaliated in the hope of taking advantage of his drink-reduced condition. George was a strong man, however, and finding himself stumbling under a frantic rain of blows from his wife he resorted to his clenched fists and knocked her to the ground. Annie was still stunned and feeling the first welling of blood inside her mouth when George exploded out into the night, cursing the world in general and Annie Collier and Nat Bardsley in particular.

Annie never saw George again.

Everything I knew about George Collier suggested that he left his home that night bent on violent revenge. He felt humiliated that he should still have to come second in his own wife's affections, to a man she knew didn't even want her.

Nat Bardsley probably let George in so as not to wake the whole street. The two men argued, one trying to quieten the other, apologize even. Nat must have turned away to go back to bed, tired of trying to rationalize with a raving drunk and believing that the man's righteous, drink-fuelled ranting had burnt itself out. On hearing a clatter and sensing a rush of air behind him, Nat turned straight into the scything sweep of the razor-sharp cleaver that George Collier swung at him. The blade struck deep, Nat's throat was sliced through and he sank back onto the stairs, amazed as the life poured from his body.

Panic-stricken, and probably sobering up rapidly now in the full realization of what he'd done, George Collier fled the scene of the crime. He did not return to Weatherfield for the best part of a year; long after Bernard Cartwright had taken the blame for the killing and the case was closed.

When Annie heard the news of Nat's murder the following morning in Cartwright's – despite her initial devastation – she soon put two and two together. Her husband still hadn't come home and the object of his jealous hatred, and her passionate obsession, lay dead. On top of that, the mark of Annie's own hand was plainly scored across the dead man's face. Did that make her party to the murder? Would George come looking for her now to ensure her silence? Would he even try to lay the blame on her, saying that she had killed Nat in their quarrel and then tried to frame her husband? Whatever she felt on hearing the news, fear kept Annie Collier's mouth tight shut until Jack Medlock found her hiding in her brother's house in the quiet little town of Kingston in upstate New York.

Alice Cartwright stole the only time she could find to go to Nat's house and try to apologize for her earlier lack of faith in their love. Alice was naturally upset to have heard the rumour of a romantic liaison between Nat and Annie Collier and she'd acted in haste. She would tell him so. Alice and Nat's love would surely prove stronger than factory workers' gossip or any minor misunderstanding between the two of them. She knew she could be at Nat's house and back within the hour. The baby was fast asleep and Bernard would not wake. He was a heavy sleeper. It was a crazy risk but she had to take it.

The sight of Nat Bardsley's blood-soaked corpse on the back stairs of the butcher's shop plunged Alice Cartwright into a deep abyss of shock and madness from which she was never to escape. In a state of stunned and floundering distress she must have picked up the bloody meat-cleaver in disbelief. How long she sat there before her husband found her and took her away from the horrific scene, we can never know. At some point she found and clung on to the gypsy good-luck charm that the blade had detached from its permanent place around her lover's neck. It remained clutched in Alice's fist until the moment of her death, when it fell to the kitchen floor to lay undisturbed until Jack Medlock picked it up.

The rest we know. After the trip to see Annie in America, as Jack Medlock began to peel away the layers of confusion he himself had helped to provide, the truth must have chilled him to the bone. In Jack's own mind, it was vital now that he should see justice done for the sake of all three dead; Alice, Nat and Bernard Cartwright himself. He had sworn to deal square with Bernard, whatever that took. He must have felt, under the circumstances, that recourse to the law was not an option.

Jack Medlock tracked the activities of George Collier and his criminal associates throughout the winter months of 1899 leading into 1900. The illegal barge transportation racket that George was party to was slowly being dismantled by the determined efforts of Jack and his men but it seemed that George had developed a slippery skin when it came to his likely apprehension for any misdemeanour. Whenever the police net closed in, George always managed to slip through untouched.

On the night of 15 January 1900, Jack Medlock was off duty. His friend, Jim Hadfield, was occupied by certain medical matters that very night in a modified cow-shed on the outskirts of Weatherfield, re-fitting the right ear of a struggling pugilist on whom he'd laid a considerable stake. Jim had expected to see Jack at the fight as there was information to be had regarding the whereabouts of the lady mayoress's recently stolen jewellery. But Jack Medlock never appeared. Jim later told his friend that he'd missed an epic match and that the doctor's timely handiwork with needle and thread had helped realize a healthy return on a number of large wagers, including Jim's own.

Whether Jack had arranged a meeting with George Collier on some dubious pretext that night, or whether he simply knew the man's every move, we cannot say. Sometime, though, late on the night of 15 January or in the early hours of the 16th, Jack Medlock confronted the man he believed to be responsible for the deaths of three misguided but nevertheless innocent people.

George Collier knew that Jack could never hope to prove his involvement in the Cartwright business. He must have laughed in the policeman's face as they spoke of it. Yet that laugh must have caught in his throat once he realized what Medlock was proposing.

A fight. Here and now. No weapons, just fists. The winner walks away and the affair is ended for good. George Collier must have thought this outwardly calm little copper was some kind of lunatic. This wasn't exactly an orthodox approach to policing in George's experience. And George was a hard man; not big but stocky and powerful and he was no observer of any fancy Marquis of Queensberry regulations when it came to a scrap.

The two men removed their jackets. Nobody ever commented in the course of the investigation into George Collier's death that it seemed unusual that his coat was found on the low tow-path wall, neatly folded as though he'd momentarily laid it to one side.

Where the one combatant was nasty and vicious, the other was cool and methodical. George may have been a handful around the streets and pubs of Weatherfield but in fighting terms, Jack was from a different world. He had studied many things during his time on the police force but the subject that had been addressed most assiduously was this one. A fight was a scientific study for Jack Medlock, a detached and dispassionate exercise whereby an aggressor's strength and will would be systematically dismantled and sooner or later rendered totally impotent. Jack could be persuaded to admit that his leisure time at the illegal ringside may have been misspent but he would never have said it was wasted.

At some point, George Collier caught Jack a sickening blow to the left eye that must have opened a flow of blood that temporarily rendered the eye useless. To Jack this was merely a cause for minor tactical readjustment. Soon George Collier's face was cut to ribbons; mouth blooded, eyes closed by swelling and nose shattered.

Maybe Collier fell into the canal and drowned as one last blow took all the fight from his body. If so, Jack Medlock left him to fend for himself. Maybe that last, knock-out blow left Collier unconscious on the canal bank, right at the edge of the water. If so Jack Medlock's final act of vengeance, on behalf of those he saw as wronged, was a cold one indeed.

Either way, Jack Medlock walked home from the canal that night having found at least some semblance of peace in his troubled soul. He had done a terrible wrong. He had done it for Alice, for Bernard and for Nat Bardsley. The Cartwright Case was closed at last.

Weatherfield, Summer 2000

What remains of the Cartwright story? Only Amelia survived to take the line on into the twentieth century and beyond. Nat Bardsley has no living relative that I have yet been able to trace and Jack Medlock is remembered now only by his daughter Martha and those few readers still prepared to blow the dust from his memoirs.

The only other line to prosper after the events of our story was the Hadfields, some of whom still hold prominent positions in Weatherfield and who count amongst their numbers a well-known politician, an opera singer and a serious novelist. No doctors, apparently, or for that matter, boxers.

I felt I'd come to know all those people whose stories had touched on that of Bernard Cartwright, the man whose fate initiated my investigation and so, on a warm day in May, I decided to try to find them and, in a way, complete the journey that started with the rumour, spread around Coronation Street, of the discovery of Nat Bardsley's body.

I knew that I could never hope to find a last resting-place for Nat. His body was consumed in the fires of Cartwright's boiler-room – now a long-lost part of the foundations of Weatherfield's Freshco supermarket. But I could at least try to locate the others.

Jack Medlock had fallen in love with America on that first trip there with Rose. It had been his wish to live there when his police-work was over but though, according to Martha, he talked of it endlessly, he never made it.

Jack lies alongside Rose in a corner of Holy Trinity Church, Weatherfield. Their little plot, still tidy thanks to Martha, is shaded by an elm tree that is far older than the church itself.

Behind the crumbling church wall runs the bypass that takes commuters in a constant, rushing stream towards Manchester and Liverpool. Few take the time to stop and walk there any more.

It felt strange to stand in that spot for the first time and wonder how Jack Medlock himself felt on that January night at the canalside. He must have sensed the casting out of a demon that had haunted him from another, earlier time, when, only yards away, Bernard Cartwright had begged him to 'deal square'.

Alice Cartwright's grave at St Aidan and Oswald's remains as neat now as it must have done when Amelia and Jack saw to its upkeep all those years ago. I was surprised to see fresh flowers in that same fixed vase that Amelia once used. Somebody was still looking after Alice. I had an idea as to who it might be but felt that this was one time when the story had moved outside my province.

By lunch-time I had visited both Jack and Alice. I still wondered about Bernard. What possessed me to get back in the car and go trailing up the M6 to Preston I don't know. But I did it nevertheless. Somehow it seemed like the only way to bring the story to a close.

I arrived in Preston in the middle of the afternoon and went to the Town Hall in search of any information I could find on the site of Bernard Cartwright's execution and burial. The man on the Visitor's Information desk pointed me in the right direction but he was sure the old prison building was long gone. Still, I'd come this far . . .

I didn't know whether to laugh or cry at the irony of what I discovered on that wind-swept corner of the old town. It looked like every other town centre in England – a depressingly ugly precinct and a draughty, multi-storey car-park growing out from an anonymous cluster of the same chainstores you'll find in Weatherfield, Penzance or Inverness.

On the site of the prison building where Bernard Cartwright was hanged and later buried stands a proud new outpost of Freshco's supermarket. I got back in the car and came home.

Afterword

It's been a long time since King Cotton ruled over Weatherfield. Almost all of the giant mill chimneys have gone and none of those remaining spew out black smoke the way they used to. We don't get the thick fog that I choked through on the way to school any more. It's a cleaner, brighter place than it was and I for one am grateful for it. At the same time, we no longer see the donkey-stoned front steps that demonstrated each family's pride in its own little corner. Most front doors are locked when you call these days.

Which is why I'm thankful that I've spent my life on Coronation Street. The best of what was seems to linger there, while the worst of what is seems to find no place. I hope it remains that way.

My research goes on. I still have the complete – or as near as I can manage – history of the town to write. Remarkably, no one has ever taken on the task before and I was always amazed as I trawled the shelves of libraries and bookshops that I could read about nineteenth century tap-fittings in Oldham but nothing about events in Weatherfield that shook the world (or at least prodded bits of it). I hope the situation will soon be rectified.

I had thought there could be no more twists and turns left in the Cartwright story. So much of the trouble I'd had in trying to bring it to light – finding the publishing costs, sponsorship – stemmed from misunderstandings with surviving members of the family and the kind of intolerance from others that proves that mud can stick to a family name even after a hundred years have gone by. I understand more clearly now how that can happen.

As I was wrapping up my Cartwright research and putting

the final chapters of this book together I discovered some-thing that might bring a wry smile to the face of any of Bernard Cartwright's descendants. It seems that George Collier – in my firm belief, though I cannot prove it, the actual murderer – was living with a woman named Edna Yates at the time of his death. Six months after George's body was pulled from the canal, Edna gave birth to a child, Margaret who she gave up for adoption in the autumn of 1900. The child grew up to marry a Barlow in the late 1920s – he was my own father's cousin.

It seems that I have a distant and long-dead relative who, though it can never definitively be proved, was a notorious criminal and brutal murderer. Though I feel duty-bound to reveal this to the reader, I can only hope Fred Elliott does not venture this far into my concluding notes. I have yet to inform him.

As I began to file away the myriad notes and cuttings that pertain to the Cartwright Case I began to feel that a hundred years – though still only a few generations – in terms of all that has passed through the world between now and then, repre-sents a huge chasm between myself sitting poring over notebooks in a computer-equipped library and the actual events in the Weatherfield of 1897. I was not there and I have not met a soul who was, so I acknowledge that I can never be sure – nobody can – about what really happened from moment to moment on the night of the deaths or indeed after-wards. All the witnesses are long dead and the story lives on only in yellowing papers and sepia photographs. I have presented my interpretation and nothing more. Aspects of it may prove inaccurate under a forensic microscope – we hope more focused than that of James Campbell Hadfield – but that is for others to judge. Indeed the aforementioned doctor's own taste for lurid fiction may have muddied the factual waters such that there is no longer any hope of them settling back to a clarity from which a researcher could ever benefit.

Nothing will alter the fact that Bernard Cartwright was found guilty of murder and hanged. Just as in the later Jack the Ripper case, the conjectures in this volume will no doubt swiftly be followed by a learned counter-blast, based on the same painstakingly accumulated materials, detailing that Bernard was, in fact, a psychopath with a death-wish who fooled the world. I look forward to reading it. After all, when I was a teacher I always made a point of telling my students to beware of anyone who regaled them with 'the truth'. I see no reason to change that view now.

Afterthought

During the course of my general work in exploring the history of Weatherfield I have stumbled across a number of stories that, like the Cartwright Case, appear to have presented a puzzle that time has yet to resolve. I only hope that time will afford me the opportunity to explore them further once the full History is completed.

Two sets of incidents in particular I found to be intriguing. The first concerns the death of a young soldier from Rosamund Street who was on home leave in Weatherfield during the Second World War. His body was found in a ditch on the edge of town in February 1942. The soldier had been shot once through the back of the head. The murderer was never found. At the time, there was considerable ill-feeling in the town caused by the presence of a number of German prisoners-of-war who were being detained in a small camp on the hills close by. Rumours were rife as to the nature of the soldier's death. It was felt in some quarters that the captured Germans, mostly airmen – others were from a U-Boat sunk in Morecambe Bay – were afforded far too much freedom and sympathy. They had already caused a stir among the town's single young women with their striking looks and bearing. In the search for a scapegoat there were near-riots on the streets of Weatherfield but nobody ever came forward with enough evidence to unearth a culprit. The soldier, a corporal in the Lancashire Fusiliers was in line for a gallantry decoration after a heroic action in North Africa. He was one of only a handful of survivors and it is ironic that he should come through the storm of all-out desert war to be killed by a murderer's bullet in his own home town.

The second story concerns a well-known pop music promoter of the Sixties whose body was discovered floating in the Red Rec lake on the morning after the Beatles played in Weatherfield for the first and only time. I had attended the concert myself – 18 November 1963 – and remember the furore the morning after all but eclipsing the hysteria of the night before. There was talk of drugs, rock 'n' roll excess and a possible suicide pact. For a brief period, Weatherfield was the centre of the media universe but as nothing was ever resolved, the circus soon moved on to far more resonant world affairs in the wake of the Kennedy assassination.

Two fascinating stories from Weatherfield's past – both of them unsolved mysteries for future investigation.

ACKNOWLEDGEMENTS

I am grateful for the assistance and support of everyone at the *Weatherfield Gazette*, Weatherfield Libraries and Leisure Service and the Records Office of Weatherfield Magistrate's Court.

I would like to thank the countless good people of Weatherfield and beyond who so readily contributed their time, their photographs, their memories and above all their abiding spirit of friendship.

Special thanks go to Roy Cropper and Fred Elliott. And of course, thanks always, to Deirdre.

Finally, I must thank all my friends on Coronation Street who have supported me in this work. I owe you all a drink in the Rovers. The only pity is that Alice, Bernard, Nat and Jack can't join us and tell their stories for themselves.

Ken Barlow
Weatherfield, July 2000